A SENTIMENTAL NOVEL

OTHER WORKS BY ALAIN ROBBE-GRILLET
IN ENGLISH TRANSLATION

The Erasers

The Voyeur

Jealousy

In the Labyrinth

For a New Novel

La Maison de Rendez-Vous

Project for a Revolution in New York

Topology of a Phantom City

Recollections of the Golden Triangle

Djinn

Ghosts in the Mirror

Why I love Barthes

A SENTIMENTAL NOVEL

ALAIN ROBBE-GRILLET

TRANSLATED BY D.E. BROOKE

Originally published in French as *Un roman sentimental*
by Fayard, Paris in 2007

Copyright ©2007 by Fayard
Translation and translator's preface ©2013 by D. E. Brooke

First edition, 2014
All rights reserved

Library of Congress Cataloging-in-Publication Data

Robbe-Grillet, Alain, 1922-2008.
 [Roman sentimental. English]
 A sentimental novel / Alain Robbe-Grillet ; translated by D. E. Brooke.
   pages cm
 ISBN 978-1-62897-006-7 (pbk. : alk. paper)
 I. Brooke, D. E., translator. II. Title.
 PQ2635.O117R6613 2014
 843'.914--dc23
              2014001112

Partially funded by the Illinois Arts Council, a state agency
and by the University of Illinois at Urbana-Champaign

The publication of this work was supported by the grant
from the Centre national du livre (CNL)

www.dalkeyarchive.com

Cover: design and composition by Mikhail Iliatov
Printed on permanent/durable and acid-free paper

TRANSLATOR'S PREFACE   7

A SENTIMENTAL NOVEL   13

TRANSLATOR'S PREFACE

ALAIN ROBBE-GRILLET'S NOVEL *Un roman sentimental* was published in France in October 2007. Less than six months later, on the 18th of February 2008, Robbe-Grillet was dead. This last book, ending a writing and filmmaking career that spanned almost six decades, was more or less roundly dismissed as an obscene book, written by an octogenarian possibly no longer in his right mind. On a French television show from 2007, the interviewer asked the author if, like Apollinaire's notorious pornographic novel *Les Onze Mille Verges, A Sentimental Novel* is not simply a literary curiosity. After expressing justified indignation at the comparison, Robbe-Grillet replied that, to his way of thinking, every work is a literary curiosity, "*La Jalousie* was a literary curiosity." Curiosity or not, it seems odd that this last work by the man dubbed "the pope of the new novel" should be deemed so devoid of merit as to be of no interest to the American literary establishment, but an editor at the French publisher Fayard confirms that, indeed, all their publishing contacts in the U.S. turned the book down in 2007 due to its subject matter, which was considered beyond the pale. This pious exhibition of moral opprobrium can be classified as wrongheaded, springing from a comfort zone of profound and habitual moral hypocrisy.

The novel purports to transform into a work of literary fiction the author's own avowed catalog of perverse fantasies, which he claimed had remained unchanged since the age of twelve, and that he had been making notes of over the years, every one consisting of transgressions perpetrated against young girls. In the course of 239 numbered paragraphs, and in a series of theatrical set pieces evoked in sumptuous detail, we read about fourteen-year-old Gigi and her education by her father (also her lover) in matters erotic, more specifically sado-masochistic, with the assistance and participation of a chorus of female children who are submitted to progressively more excruciating, savage and brutal acts of torture and rape—the reader is spared no detail of organs lacerated, blood spilled, fluids propagated. There are also digressions in the form of flashbacks and asides that fill in the story of this or that sundry character, each producing its own mini hair-raising fable within the story.

The unusual coupling of the style that Robbe-Grillet pioneered in the new novel with the telling of this traditional libertine novel—that form wherein an episodic tale consists principally of successive scenes and encounters culminating in orgasms for one or more characters—proves felicitous, achieving a Brechtian effect of distantiation.[1] The close-up descriptions of the machinery of torture—the pulleys and winches and their operation, the materiality of the gruesome dildos, seats of nails, the multiple suspended parallel blades that penetrate flesh, the virgins strung up in a circle by their feet, or the redheads fed to rabid dogs—all in polished, almost scientific language, with no hint of a moral dimension, produce an unholy kind of terror and pity and firmly relegate these scenes to the realm of the unreal from which they came. This feeling of unreality is furthered by the relentless mounting intensity of the cruelties.

The only reference to any world outside of this setting is the description of a global economy whose elaborate rules and regulations, tariffs and taxes, aim at collecting wealth, either to maintain social status, or to support a corrupt state or government whose interest in money is rivaled only by its own complicity and participation in the perpetration of sexual torture. The socio-economic world of the book might not stand up to scrutiny as a model republic, but it does, overall, reflect Robbe-Grillet's mistrust of laws, authority, and righteousness.

In case the reader might imagine that the book is a one-note tale of grim horror, it is important to mention that, odd though it may appear, lighter touches do abound. There is tenderness between the girls, as well as in the development of the father-

---

1 "All my books are Brechtian, at least in this sense," the author tells a skeptical interviewer, stating that this is how he aspires to produce that terrifying and salutary state of catharsis as prescribed by Aristotle in his Poetics.

daughter relationship, even as Gigi submits to, or with her father's collusion delivers, gruesome punishments. The nature of the tenderness seen in this world, constructed on relationships of power and domination, is subject to willing submission to the infliction of suffering that is not only prized, but is also its own reward—for having been paid such attention. And left behind is always some material proof of this rare and true generosity and intimacy: a bruise, a blister, or any such souvenir.

Admittedly, such favors are only bestowed on the females in this tale. When questioned on this point, Robbe-Grillet gamely replied that he purported to catalog his own sexual fantasies, not the world's lexicon of all possible passions. Presumably, he would give the same answer if faulted for the astoundingly clichéd nature of the descriptions of the girls—dressed in lace, ruffles, and corsets, their flat stomachs, shapely breasts, and slender long legs too often reminiscent of a *Victoria's Secret* catalog.

At times, Robbe-Grillet is clearly having fun—in assigning a rhyming riddle of absurdly cute names to the little slave girls picked up at the boarding school, or in the picaresque strands of the story, such as the appearance of Sexie hidden between the blankets in the carriage, making her escape, the exotic denomination of sultanes, Gigi's weird and hilarious post-orgy interaction with Gil the cook and sodomizer, or the little girls smothering cake all over their faces. While it might seem that innocence has no place in such a story, in fact it does: without it, its desecration would not have the punch it packs. The nightmare can be summoned only in inverse proportion to the innocence of the victims on whom horror is inflicted.

Throughout the book, minutiae of painterly detail and the pristine clarity of the language make settings explode in full cinemascope and Technicolor. The author controls the light, the sound, the shading, the décor and spatial contours, the chiaroscuros, planes and curves. The architectural details and furnishings of each room or location are conveyed with a mastery of technique much like an impeccable master cinematographer painting with light. Robbe-Grillet's aesthetic treatment, lush and sumptuous, is troublingly pleasing, producing a densely visual literary artifact, even when the material described is gut-wrenching.

Two bookends are employed to frame the main portion of the novel. The first places an unknown narrator in a space that is blank, white, unknown, devoid of all specificity—a void, a vacuum. This is precisely how, in his 1991 memoir, *Ghosts in the Mirror*, Robbe-Grillet describes his impressions upon finishing reading Camus's *The Stranger*, a reading he claims transformed his relationship to the world and prompted him to give up his career as an agronomist to become a novelist.[2]

The placing of the unnamed narrator in the same white space at the outset of *A Sentimental Novel*, signals that talismanic power of writing that will be unleashed when we leave the space of the vacuum womb and its menace of looming catastrophe, to inhabit the world of the imagination. The peculiar endnote—the closing segment of the framing device—a fable about little girls who live underwater, told to friends by a little girl in a dark attic, playfully evokes the mood of fairy tales and nursery rhymes and looking glass worlds: a pointed reminder that all this is made-up nonsense

---

[2] Robbe-Grillet ascribes his decision to quit his job as an agronomist in order to write to his, by his own admission, extremely idiosyncratic reading of Camus's The Stranger. The murder Mersault commits in the novel is, for Robbe-Grillet, the result of a certain situation, which is the situation of the world. There is, on one hand, the chaos of the world, on the other, the inner void of me. Not filling the void results in an eventual implosion, like Mersault's, not as a result of something within, but because of the invasiveness of the nature of the world beyond, its chaos, its vast disorder (in The Stranger, the sea, the sun). Talismanic, writing harnesses the world. Or so concludes Robbe-Grillet. To fail to write, to bring order to this chaos results in catastrophe. Examined in this light, his rejection of the 19th century novel's narrative style and structure makes sense. He decried as factitious the provision of arbitrarily selected facts, presented as a narrative of truths, fixed and immutable. He protested this very immutability—exemplified by the simple past tense and the third person narrative voice—as being the opposite of life, of the multiplicity of reality, its myriad facets and shifting forms. That form was, in fact, death.

In search of a more authentic language with which to articulate experience, he arrives at his precise, pictorial manner of depicting material reality, along with an apparent, constant, intentional highlighting and dismantling

acting as a distraction from the horrors so recently inflicted on the reader.

If writing is an attempt at making sense of one's strange relationship to the world, this final venture by Robbe-Grillet to harness and convey the material sent forth by his unconscious appears an even more heroic undertaking. A shrewd man, he might have chosen not to publish this book, or to have it appear pseudonymously, aware of the condemnation it would provoke. So, one might wonder: had he taken leave of his senses? To which the answer might be that yes, in a sense, he had abandoned "sense" in the order of the world. Instead he opted for the order of literature and to apply his arsenal of skills, honed over a decades-long career, to organize and structure, and then voluntarily relinquish, a secret world that had been his alone for all the world to see. The uttering of taboos might appear to unleash the terrifying power of nightmares, but such a transformation of haunting horrors into a work of literature is an act of existential alchemy. The horror that is unspoken festers behind the veils of decency and order, of the righteous and the law—it perpetrates wrongs that cannot be righted.

of the machinery of narrative that had previously been painstakingly shielded from the reader. Often repeating scenes, his books unmoor the reader in relation to time and space, the loose strands of storyline proposing a sort of puzzle, affecting to make the reader a co-conspirator with whom to solve the story, uncover truth, as it were.

In fact, and notwithstanding his reputation as the chief prophet of this new form of objective novel writing, Robbe-Grillet rode a thin line, arguably never fully subscribing to the theories of the new novel. He writes of "the deviousness of the writer's text" and refers to his writing style ("my own so-called neutrality") as a whitewash. He recognizes that to tell any form of a story, to write, is to justify a particular elevation of certain facts and notions, the particular privileging of one narrative over another. Ultimately what livens his works is the precarious balancing of these two forces that produce fragile spaces where the unruly drifting hum of the unconscious—the very engine prompting him to write—is, if not articulated, entirely audible and unpredictable, often terrorizing. What is spectacular about this novel is the ascendance of the contents of the unconscious and its coincidence with the style that originally allowed Robbe-Grillet to tackle the external world.

A SENTIMENTAL NOVEL

1. At first sight, the place in which I find myself is neutral, white, so to speak; not dazzlingly white, rather of a non-descript hue, deceptive, ephemeral, altogether absent. If there were something to see in front of me, it could be seen without any difficulty under this uniform lighting that is neither excessive nor stingy, stripped, in the final analysis, of all adjectivity. Inside a space such as this, unconvincingly asserting its indifference, it is neither hot nor cold.

2. The only problem, on reflection, is of a different order altogether: I don't know what I'm doing here, nor why I've come, with what conscious or impulsive intention, that is, if one can even speak of there having been an intention at some point… But at what point? Was I perhaps driven here by force, against my will, in spite of myself even, or something else along these lines. Am I in prison for some misdeed, offense, crime, or on the contrary, by mistake, the victim of an unfortunate identification error?

3. The room seems cubic, without any visible windows or doors, without furniture or decoration. I am motionless, lying on my back, my legs outstretched, my arm resting alongside my body, my torso slightly raised at about a twenty degree incline to the (metallic?) frame of what must be a very low profile box-spring, potentially equipped with an adjustable height function, higher than normal, hinged like those of hospital patients. So, might I be in a clinic, recovering from surgery? The thought crosses my mind that this may well be a morgue, to which my lifeless body has been transported, following some accident…

4. Something, however, just as quickly, stops me from subscribing to such a hypothesis: If I were dead, and most importantly, thus exposed to the freezing atmosphere of a funereal chamber, I would feel the cold penetrate me bit by bit. Whereas, I feel the opposite sensation: the rising warmth of a bower, and very

soon of heat even, and rainforest-like exhalations, whose damp and heavy blasts besiege me, disorientate me, invade me. In my torpor, I believe I am seeing the diffuse light of the walls that surround me moving, as though the sun, filtered by the leaves of immense trees teeming overhead with an indistinct murmur, were alighting on land (and on me) in the form of a haze of particles without definite contours, without direction, without plans.

5. Towards the back wall, the one on which my languorous eyes alight most easily, I distinguish, in the foreground of a picture that is quickly revealed to be a forest landscape of vertical and rectilinear trunks, a sort of basin of water so clear it becomes almost immaterial, an oblong widening of a limpid spring, deep as a bathtub or deeper even, set between gray rounded rocks, soft to the touch, welcoming. A girl is sitting there on a stone polished with age, which to her represents the ideal bench, the water's edge where her long legs dangle in the blue mirrored swirls of this lovely nymphæum, as natural as it is picturesque, whose temperature must be identical to the air, and to the feminine charms themselves, undulating, liquid already, above the moving mirror and its unforeseen shivers.

6. The swimmer is so much a part of her warm, caressing, ambrosiac environment that she dwells there unperturbed, completely naked. Barely pubescent, she is graceful, shapely, and her flesh is so white, so far from the amber expected of a native—whose savage beauty, the golden brown of caramel and quick movements like hunted prey, would suit the apparent landscape from which she emerges—so improbably milky an apparition, that one might instead think she were in a northern European bathroom, climate-controlled to the mild register of Turkish baths, its fanciful wallpaper displaying an equatorial décor.

7. The girl, languidly attending to her grooming, has raised her arms on both sides of her face. She is removing a white fluffy towel

A Sentimental Novel / 17

wrapped around her head like a sort of turban, slowly releasing her hair, whose pale golden tresses fall on her shoulders that she shrugs lightly to tidy the supple curls, finally raising eyes of an azure to match her personification of the beautifully fair girl child, innocent and fragile. Did she, briefly, lower her lids toward me, for a fleeting instant?

8. But then a man's voice is heard calling from outside, nearby, imperiously: "Angina!" Or more precisely, "Ann-djinn-a," in a vaguely Anglo-Saxon pronunciation that, at least, dispels unfortunate confusion with the name of a malady. This, evidently, is the bather's first name, because, still holding the towel, she promptly raises her face, turning toward the wall to her right. This might be her father, or another older relative, who, from an adjacent room, is ordering her to join him in a tone that brooks no argument. At any rate, the girl complies instantly.

9. The room next door appears to be a sort of small-scale library, whose walls are entirely covered by traditional dark wooden shelves displaying no fewer than several thousand volumes, bound or not, seemingly arranged with care. The man we have assumed to be the father is standing in front of a desk, a hand rests on the book he holds open on it. In his other hand he holds a stiff rod like those used by orchestra conductors, a little longer perhaps, and more flexible. In his prime (barely forty) and tall, his stern expression accentuates the fastidious nature of this study, that might well, under other circumstances, what with its divan for repose, its cushions and low footstools, be a place of rest, of meditation, of metaphysical solitude, or even a slightly austere boudoir.

10. This character's authoritarian gaze with its troubling acuity, is focused in fact, not on the book he was reading, but beyond it, past the desk, at young Ann-Djinna, who is now kneeling about two meters away, on a prie-dieu of sculpted black wood, covered in plush red velvet padding into which just her left knee is sinking,

the other is set on the ground, and therefore lower to the side, spreading the sweet communicant's bent legs with a sensual tipping of the hips. But she is no longer naked, fortunately, because this room, less well heated than the bathroom, would not have accommodated that state without marked discomfort.

11. In her haste to obey, she has only pulled on the essentials of her prescribed costume corresponding to her present role as reader, that is, without underwear, a black frou-frou lace corset that pushes up her young breasts, whose little hard tips emerge, as do the top half of the areolas, leaving the milky skin bare from the curve of her hips to the tapering of her thighs, where gathered garters covered in minuscule roses hold up black large-mesh fishnet stockings.

12. Her bosom lifted, the curve of her arched back accentuated by the very constraining corset, in both hands she holds her open book on exactly the same page as the master, who has selected the vesperal reading. As attentive to the prosody as he is to posture, he appraises his lovely schoolgirl without the slightest indulgence, prepared to punish with a single, dry snap of his baton the smallest mistake in reading, rhythm, or even diction. The adolescent is no doubt accustomed to this scholarly exercise, whose aim is visibly educational, for a docile smile (complicit, or the product of patient dressage?) hovers constantly on her delicate, pretty features, while dainty movements of her body emphasize her trembling contours, though with modesty and discretion.

13. Based on her suitably shameful pouts, her feigned innocence, the passages murmured in a low voice, as though apologizing for the obscenity, she is nonetheless being forced to enunciate clearly, it is clear that Ann-Djinna, more often called Gigi, the diminutive dating back to her early childhood, must tonight be reading her father a passage of literary erotica, more or less scabrous, from an obscene eighteenth-century novel perhaps, whose unfolding

story she is following daily in this manner. And it is with the total compliance of a good pupil wishing to learn, to perfect herself, to correct her errors, that the studious novice, in an inevitable conclusion, submits to the customary merited punishment.

14. The scrupulous father, who has walked over to the prie-dieu where Gigi, still in the same position and in the same apparel, is now pressing her folded forearms down on the velvet armrests, makes the sweet, guilty, repentant girl repeat, several times, each of the sentences that made her performance falter, be it that she failed to respect the brief, unequal pauses marked by punctuation, or that a rarefied, unusual turn of phrase or particularly scandalous term was caught in her throat and pronounced jarringly, or that an inadequate degree of composure accompanied a lascivious overtone, a sexual cruelty, or a disgusting practice...

15. And each time, she receives a new stroke on her bottom, until achieving the precise expression of the lines in a perfect, fluid, mellifluous pronunciation of the delectable passage that she will now know by heart, rendered affectingly as ever for being spoken in her tender voice with its childish lilt. Far from cowering before the fearsome baton that her father wields skillfully, artistically distributing the scarlet lines on the two ivory globes, Gigi proffers her bruised rear by an increasingly accentuated arching of her back, as she begins to weep soundlessly, tears streaming down her pink cheeks, a protruding lip, a slightly jutting chin, heavy, childish tears that finally drop onto her hands, which are gripping the armrest, the better to bear the repeated lashes of the slender crop without wincing in pain, or in careless opposition.

16. Satisfied with her penitential zeal, moreover not wanting to compromise her natural gifts through excessive demands, and in order to console her by way of a merciful absolution for her shortcomings, her teacher kisses her paternally on her mouth, offered, trustingly, partway open, moist and sweet. Then, he stands the

victim back up—her tears have already been pacified to form a smile—nimble, agile, just barely unsteady, by holding her delicate neck in his large, virile hand, and leads her in this manner to the small, agreeable room, intended for savoring cigars and drinks, where he wants to offer her a comforting draft before going to sleep.

17. Less stiff than during the reading lesson, the man with the incisive dark eyes immediately sits, allowing himself to sink into a large tawny armchair. Without having to ask him what he wants, the girl, straight away, walks behind the old, tarnished pewter counter, readily grabs two bottles, one after the other, from the shelves covering the walls, removes ice cubes from the fridge, and half fills a shaker with them, etc. The geisha of risqué readings plays her part as corseted barmaid equally admirably, for it only takes her a couple of minutes to present, kneeling for reasons of practicality, and holding the tray very straight in both hands, his favorite cocktail to this omnipresent educator who continues to gaze at her.

18. He contemplates her for an instant, motionless, in waiting, at his feet, and pays her a sophisticated compliment on her pose as well-trained maid and on her flattering and intimate turnout as an underage courtesan, without failing to make mention, in ceremonious terms, of the numerous bright pink, distinct, artfully crisscross marks that decorate her ass. Indeed, having asked her to turn and turn again, in order to allow them to be admired from diverse angles, her tray in her hands, before kneeling in front of him, he is able to conduct a detailed inspection of them, grazing them even, with three nonchalant fingers, confirming with pleasure that the strokes delivered with the principal aim of making his delectable boudoir pupil suffer, of seeing her dissolve in tears at the conclusion of the punishment, in spite of her bravery, have also left, from the waist to the thighs, long, sensitive marks that will stay raw for several hours without, however, resulting in un-

sightly ecchymoses or edemas, or breaks in the skin, all of which, while certainly quite pleasing in the heat of the moment, require pharmaceutical care. Gigi looks down and blushes at receiving praise as it is recommended young ladies do, as soon as they instigate gallantries, desirable nudity, or sexual chastisement.

19. Then the master picks up his glass, tastes it in small sips, nods his approval, and promptly holds it out to his improvised slave, now suddenly his companion, so she might first drink what quantity suits her. Wishing to honor this favor, still kneeling obediently with her thighs spread, she raises the tall crystal goblet enclosed in her graceful hands to her lips, lifting her horizontally parted elbows in a pose of ancient ritual. The nun partaking of the sacred poison, in this manner, she reveals as an offering, at the top of her constraining corset, armpits covered in an almost invisible blond fluff that sound a troubling echo to her chaste pubic down of golden curls, displayed rather nicely under the inferior arc of the garterless corset, which ends just lower than the round of her bottom in a black muslin ruffle.

20. To better frame the tender object of desire, two lace tips on either side drop from this vaporous flounce to the top of her crotch, meeting in a heavy jay-blue gem, matched to the irises of her eyes, which makes the adolescent look like a little operetta bohemian. When her mentor deems she has drunk enough alcohol to unbind her tongue, he asks if she enjoyed the evening's reading. The girl first confesses that she found the scenes of couplings according to conjugal norms somewhat boring, repetitive, spoiled by useless crude, vulgar, and even repugnant terms. The attentive father thinks to himself that it was precisely these shocking obscenities that justified the longest series of corrective, delectable lashings.

21. His pupil had, on the other hand, very much enjoyed the great feast that lasted three days and four nights, where a victorious sultan, for the sole pleasure of his court, tortured to death the

nine hundred girls delivered the previous night as war trophies, almost all virgins, chosen among the most beautiful of a rich, conquered city. The precise description, objective, without superfluous words, of the barbaric rapes and multiple torments inflicted on these love objects in accordance with their physical traits, age, and the state of their feminine charms (the youngest having just turned nine, the oldest not yet eighteen) proved fascinating, varied, most instructive, she said, especially for the prettiest ones, submitted to progressive cruelties producing intolerable suffering throughout their bodies, but damaging them only gradually, which were extended for several days without respite before they expired.

22. The conscientious teacher, never one to lose a chance for adding to such a dedicated pupil's learning, goes on to tell her there used to exist, in all the sumptuous palaces of the Roman provinces, a few rooms especially set aside for punishing various categories of the guilty, which, furthermore, often culminated in their execution: clumsy servants, restive concubines, surplus female prisoners, newly-wed brides whose fastidious husbands contested their intact virginity, and above all, in those felicitous times, the very many little girls, or more or less pubescent adolescents, converted to the Christian faith, and thus condemned by the emperor. Lastly, there were very young women whom families wished to do away with, for no avowable reason (rivalries, jealousies, sordid machinations to do with the division of wealth or inheritances), and whom it was commodious to sell at a good price to those with a proclivity for the criminal passions.

23. This part of the house had nothing secret about it, quite the contrary. A vast room located at the heart of the noble sleeping quarters, it was called the *castigarium*, meaning the place for punishments. It consequently housed all sorts of torture devices (at times antique or exotic), spectacular installations of hoists, chains and pulleys, giant machines whose workings were so complex that

visitors always asked to see them in action. It was also known as the *fornax*, with the double etymology of high vaulted ceilings and heat worthy of an oven generated by braziers, in which there were heated to glowing incandescence an array of steel needles, pincers (enormous or very dainty, sharp, or equipped with toothed jaws), stakes of various shapes and circumferences, iron chairs with seats of delicate spirals or needle-like spikes.

24. The main space was surrounded by private rooms, the *violaria*, where the most exquisite of the young Christian women, the most shapely or most arousing, were imprisoned, awaiting future execution. The religion they had chosen against our pagan laws having vowed them to chastity, they had first to experience the fall, reduced to the condition of little whores at the mercy of the worst perverts for a couple of weeks of depravity and debauchery receiving palace guests each day, who would always accompany their rapes with delectable humiliations and torture, whence the name *deliciae* (that signifies, among other things, caprices, dissipation, and even voluptuous excess) commonly given to the pleasure dungeons that, in addition to a bed equipped with all desirable suspension rings, offered the guests at these feasts a variety of mobile hooks allowing dangling by a foot, waist, or shoulder, as well as phalluses, wooden crosses, trestles, shackles, etc.

25. On display in the Vatican museum today, there are affecting examples of these images for the edification of the faithful: a girl child of twelve with a nicely rounded bottom, kneeling before a seated man who holds her head in both hands so that she keeps his cock deep in her mouth during ejaculation, while another man is shoving a white hot poker up her ass; a slightly older girl, her charms already in bloom, also kneeling with her arms tied in the small of her arched back, thighs widespread, her bosom lifted, as an executioner with an enormous member sodomizes her, and a second man slices off the tips of her breasts. Her ecstatic eyes and her angelic face are turned toward the heavens. These future saints

are entirely undressed, as is fitting, but the men torturing them are wearing white, very proper, though somewhat short, tunics, at times stained with blood.

26. All these redemptive sacrifices and many more are listed in the works of Apuleius, Tertullian, and Juvenal. The assiduous pupil asks if such immodest courtesans, displaying their debasement, are admitted to Paradise afterwards. Her professor says yes, no doubt, as they were made to suffer sufficiently long to expiate their indecency. After a pause for reflection on this grave matter, Gigi declares that it's not right. It would be more natural that these bitches should roast in Hell for all eternity, or slightly longer even. In order to more competently discuss the subject, she would like to read, or rather, be told stories of young, luscious beauties, tortured extensively for their religion, along with all the historic details of what is done to them, and the carnal orgasms said to be mystical, which they consequently experienced, according to all the serious chroniclers. Emboldened by mild intoxication, the audacious neophyte would like to know, moreover, if a virgin sodomized without restraint, by force or consensually, can still claim to be a virgin. But it is now time to go and rest in the great conjugal bed that the schoolgirl has shared with her beloved papa since her mother's mysterious and premature death when she was four years old.

27. After this calamity, unfathomable to her, the little girl would wake every night howling in terror. She had horrible recurring nightmares in such rapid succession that Doctor Muller, the old family doctor, suggested this solution: that she should, from then on, sleep as near to the reassuring protection of her father as possible. And Gigi herself, like a little animal, acquired the habit of curling up against this warm and vigorous body that would chase away demons. At puberty, several fruitless attempts were made to assign a separate room to her. But the grown child was not even able to doze off in them. So she turned fifteen still spending the

night, often entirely naked, in her mommy and daddy's bed, in fact, the bed of her father, teacher, and absolute master and unflagging pedagogue. Thus, her intelligence, her learning, her unusual sensibility evolved at an exceptional pace. And her slumber was cradled by sweet dreams.

28. When she opens her eyes the next morning, daylight has long broken and the sun is pouring in through the large bay windows overlooking the grounds, whose heavy curtains are not drawn. Her father, dressed in rather loose black pajamas, is lying next to her and watching her. He is in the same placid pose as King Sardanapalus in the Delacroix painting, which is further evoked by the imposing proportions of the sumptuous lair, his chest is halfway lifted against a mound of thick cushions where he leans on an elbow, pensively stroking his short beard. The girl before him is entirely naked, as always in summer heat waves. She has even thrown the sheets off to the foot of the bed. While entirely awake, she is not moving, she too, is pensive, but is sprawled on her back, limbs akimbo, her young flesh and intimate charms of a girl in bloom exposed unabashedly.

29. Her master cannot help but unreservedly admire their perfection and their grace. As for her other side, hidden by her position, he confirmed, while she was laying on her stomach a quarter of an hour earlier, that the whip marks have already almost disappeared, without any need of a soothing salve. He finally speaks: "Did you have sweet dreams, you lazy child?" Gigi replies drowsily that, in fact, she is barely emerging from a series of dream episodes that were more strange than sweet... She was sitting on a toilet seat, completely naked, but with her hands tied behind her back. A man in black was leaning over her who had the same features as her father, with a more smiling expression, mocking perhaps. Although it was very bright, he held a lit candle that he moved closer to one of her breasts, as if to better observe its stiff areola. The flame was actually so close to her flesh that the pink tip of

her tit was sizzling, starting, very quickly, to catch fire. She was experiencing an intense emotion as a result, closer to surprise than to fear or suffering, and only said in a low voice, "Can't you see, Father, that I am on fire?"

30. The martyrdom of Sankt Giesela in the eleventh century in Cologne, evoked the previous evening in the smoking room, must have left a trace. And even more so, evidently, in the rest of the dream, the tale of the virgins delivered to the conquering sultan as war trophies, twenty of whom had perished dismembered: their legs ripped apart progressively, pulled by two horizontal hand-cranked winches, while they were continually raped by ever more monstrous members, human or artificial, that tore their vaginas to the uterus, only then were their arms ripped off. The sleeper, emerging from the lavatory, still feeling the same bizarre need to urinate (a circle of lit candles had prevented her from sitting on the toilet seat) had returned to a torture chamber, as per ancient custom adjacent to the *fornax*. And in there it was really just too hot, even naked.

31. Splayed spread-eagled on the great bed, in the hope of cooling down, there were now three men in black around her, painstakingly inspecting her vulnerable nakedness, trembling in its helplessness and apprehension. They were talking among themselves, as doctors do in conference, gesticulating to designate certain parts of her anatomy that they would palpate or pinch between their thumb and index fingers. When they stuffed their fingers inside her vulva, she wanted to fight them, but then realized her limbs were incapable of movement, held tightly by four winches at the four corners of the bed, that were, with increasing strength, pulling on the chains attached to her wrists and ankles by black leather cuffs.

32. Her thighs were spread so excessively that the fragile skin was ripping in places, at the back of her knee, along her groins, on her

perineum, and her joints were starting to rip apart. A preoccupied looking practitioner was manhandling her clitoris, swollen from the rubbing and squeezing. The sensations of tearing and burning were like those on a toilet seat, but infinitely more violent, and irradiating in aggressive waves throughout her taut, illuminated body on the point of fainting. Two gentlemen in black unceremoniously spread the lips of her cunt while the third buried a far-too-large, humped object inside her slit, which she thought might be the statuette of the Virgin usually on old Doctor Muller's desk. In the paroxysms of a frightening orgasm, she suddenly began to pee, in spasmodic spurts.

33. Her pajama-clad initiator first congratulates the raped schoolgirl for having taken the precaution of remembering the unfolding of her sacrificial dream promptly after the final penetration that woke her. This allowed her to recount it in quasi-intact order with all its repetitions and contradictions. He can, moreover, attest to its happy ending, whose preliminaries he observed, as well as the tinkling, in the realm of the visible. The whole thing, naturally, took a much shorter interval of clock time, beginning with the girl's furtive caresses to her budding breasts, then the firmer fondling of the base of her *mons pubis*, until a complete orgasm, a classic masturbatory model, the only thing he could not know was whether this young, strictly monitored prisoner had performed so successfully because she had been experimenting in secret and had already honed the process (for which she would have to be severely punished), or whether today was a grand premiere, which does happen frequently during sleep, for girls as it does for boys.

34. As for the clear liquid, whose jerky spurts had seeped onto the dainty fingers slipped on top of her vulva, this was not a case of incontinent urination: Gigi, feeling the sheet under her pubis, notes the far-too-negligible quantity for a supposedly long-constrained need to urinate. This transparent mini-ejaculation accompanying orgasm is a phenomenon known to sexologists, it is

not unusual in certain adolescents girls who are prettily designated fountain fillies. "You are therefore not entitled to a supplementary spanking," he concludes, "for having peed in bed." Delighted by her father's imperturbable austerity, this same father who, in dreams, had just brought her to her first real orgasm, the schoolgirl is overcome by an irresistible rush of tenderness: she rolls toward him and kisses him all over his face. He disengages with a clumsy gesture. "Up," he says, "you lazy, Christian, whore child, and get breakfast going!"

35. Gigi, whose education is old-fashioned, founded on absolute submission to a master (a boss, lover or husband), the respect of parents, daily domestic duties, and systematic corporal punishment, even in the absence of identifiable wrongdoing, deems it perfectly normal to be the servant of a man who has personally seen to her literary, scientific, and moral education, not to mention the solid rudiments of Latin and Greek, the practice of German, and a working knowledge of philosophy from Spinoza to Hegel and his progenitors, thus sparing her an obligatory public education, such as at a religious boarding school. As for the incessant "examinations" of the paternal system that are an improvement on all diplomas and entrance exams, their indecent, libertine, and manifestly sexual nature would certainly shock many modern psychologists. These improper interrogations, trials, and punishments have, however, fashioned the awakening flesh and curious mind of the little girl who now submits to them compliantly, with fervor, gratitude, fascination, even in pain and in tears, to the point of no longer being able to go without them, daily counting her blessings for still attending such a good school.

36. The fact remains that her inflexible director of conscience and libido, delighted by the results obtained, prefers to undertake certain household chores, for some unknown reason, relegated to women: the preparation, for instance, of meals or collations. The kitchen, that also serves as a small dining room, the larger one set

aside for festive ceremonial dinners with guests, is a very bright room, by day as by night, sizeable nevertheless, with a constant air flow that averts excessive heat or humidity produced by the ovens, the washing machine, water boiling in a pot, the charcoal grill, and that evacuates odors and smoke. In here, therefore, Gigi is dressed.

37. She is perched this morning on a rustic wood and straw chair at a rectangular table, where she has set her schoolbook on the traditional Jouy waxed tablecloth adorned with mythological motifs. Enveloped in a sort of very loose, pale blue *djellaba*, casually unfastened at the neck, that bares a satin shoulder, she is revising an oceanography lesson while her father prepares red pepper scrambled eggs. She is very hungry after her night of amorous initiation. She asks, "What exactly does the word '*échancrure*' mean?" Without leaving his frying pan and spatula, the chef replies, "It is a nook hollowed by the sea in an embankment, but also the low neckline of a dress intended to reveal to the concupiscent gaze of others the appetizing flesh of the shoulders and breasts."—"So, what does the root "*chancre*" represent then?"—"An alteration of the Latin *cancer*, designating several species of carnivorous, marine crustaceans, crabs in particular, that carve out, using their pincers, in order to feed on them, certain tender, especially delicious morsels of the bodies of girls hurled from atop cliffs, the traditional immolation for appeasing the libidinal gods of the abyss. Reference, *Le Voyeur*, page 88 of the complete edition."—"Me, I could eat a whole baby quail snatched alive from its nest," murmurs the starving child in a low, muffled, interior voice.

38. So as to commit to memory the precious references she has just acquired, the diligent little pupil scribbles a few succinct notes in her schoolbook. But, the nurturing father, who is adding the final touches to his confection, which promises to be spicy, suggests serving this morning's breakfast outdoors as the predicted heat is as yet not unbearable at this hour. "What do you think?" She an-

swers with a pretty smile of happy acquiescence. "It shall be as you decide," she says, closing her book again after tagging the page with a publisher's bookmark that is a threatening, enormous wave about to break. The small dining room opens onto an exterior space like a patio, that forms a natural extension to it: an open-air quadrilateral surrounded by a covered arcade, small columns with sculpted capitals supporting a succession of archways in the manner of cloisters at a convent. But in place of the traditional geometric flowerbeds, a pool of running water of about twelve meters by eight occupies the whole central portion. Flecked gold fish in red, yellow, and black, shimmer in the clear, shallow water, abruptly breaking their monastic immobility with rapid, zigzag motions. One extremity of their domain, where the water grows deeper, offers several clusters of submerged aquatic plants of various sizes: there they can sleep in utter quietude, hide, make love, lay their eggs, eat their young, etc.

39. At the other extremity, where the water is no deeper than ten centimeters, in guise of a fountain, there sits an adolescent mother, whose white marble nakedness has, in parts, turned green, accentuating her intimate furrows and undulations. Perched on a rock above the fictitious lake that has been lost in nature, her feet rest among the bank's rounded pebbles, while her welcoming thigh forms a sweet, horizontal prop for the flat belly of a kneeling little girl, also completely naked, her legs wide apart in order to feel more stable on the uneven surface (the water, particularly shallow here, barely covers her heels and calves) who, her face raised toward the juvenile, compassionate wet-nurse, is hoisting herself to reach, with her mouth, a jutting breast, so swollen with milk it is almost spherical, whose nipple she is sucking... Bizarrely, the poor captive Ondine's arms are tied behind her back, therefore incapable of feeding herself, her very young mummy must breastfeed her on the sly.

40. This tightly handcuffed little girl, already plump in all the right places, is arching her spine to push back her bottom. This, how-

ever, we soon discover, is not the purpose of her seductive posture (her anus and vulva can be divined in the cleft). In fact, she is attempting, primarily, to push her pubis forward between her spread thighs for fear of sullying them. For she is in the process of peeing, the powerful spasmodic stream drops to the pool's surface in a silvered cascading splash. One wonders, naturally, about the rather rarefied subject staged in this fanciful allegory, the urinated water seemingly emanating from an immediate transformation of comforting milk drunk at the mammary. Might this be a lesser-known episode of Greek or Germanic legend? What interpretation might there be for it in reference books? What might the ties be that bind these two lovely nymphs? Are we, here, discovering a lineage of parthenogenetic females who breastfeed each other? And why is it that the younger one's hands are not free? Perhaps, having escaped from a nearby penitentiary, she has sought refuge amid the high reeds of swamps where the dogs chasing her dared not venture, her companions now are found but remain, alas, incapable of undoing the secret lock of the chains that restrain her...

41. Gigi, seated at the table under the arches, is eating, with gusto, the substantial serving, yellow sprinkled with red, that has just been served to her, careful, however, not to betray an unseemly voracity. Her master, returning next with a steaming *café au lait*, bread, and apricot jam, announces, as though it were an ordinary event, that his friend Sorel, whom Gigi has often seen at the house, will be stopping by in a minute to bring her a gift they have chosen together without telling her: a life-sized doll. "Why the unexpected gift?" she asks, looking surprised. "To celebrate your birthday." "But it's not my birthday at all!" "It is! Think: you are exactly fourteen and a half... And your night last night was memorable." The girl, caught off guard by this reminder, blushes, looks down at her toast, piled too high, managing just in time to catch a dribble of food with the tip of her tongue.

42. But already Sorel is walking through the main entrance to the patio accompanied by three movers in overalls carefully carrying a

long, heavy and voluminous, apparently very solid box of golden cardboard. Setting it down in front of Gigi without the slightest bump, (the giant doll must be made of porcelain,) they stand the precious parcel vertically on its smallest side. The lid, about a meter fifty by fifty centimeters, which from top to bottom forms the anterior side of the box, is held shut by an enormous red shiny ribbon, tied in a bow as per custom where gift packages are concerned. Sorel, wearing an undeniably elegant white suit, bows to the mistress of the house with all the respect due to young ladies, then turns toward the golden chest, which imperceptibly shifts on its base (the zealous deliverymen having left already), and with a single gesture, he unties the knot placed halfway up, letting the cover and the ribbon fall.

43. Inside, protected on all sides by a thick padding of pink silk, is an adolescent girl, standing, quite alive in the mischievousness of her expression and her green kittenish eyes, dressed (if one can call it that) in strips of dirty rags that are at odds with her art-object packaging. Ordered to submit to an inspection by her new owner, she emerges, taking a few dainty steps out of her box, bewitchingly gracefully. It is now easier to see that her tattered rags, stained with blood where they need to be, far from being pitiful, are in fact ripped with precision out of a light, gauzy, translucid muslin, whose frayed strips sway at the slightest breath of air. She brings to mind little Alice, photographed by Lewis Carroll, but the erotic character of her improbable pauper's outfit is more marked here, and its sadism distinctly declared.

44. As soon as she moves slightly, the judicious scissor-cut slits reveal her honey thighs all the way to the groins, streaked on the inside with bright red lash marks of an artful makeup, a naked breast, its curve already provocative, it too split crosswise by the whip, panties extremely diminutive in size, a white lace triangle, stained at its nerve center with fresh blood, spread widely, more scarlet than natural, a sanctuary staged so as to more than fore-

shadow around the wound the dark curls of a pubic muff, indeed present. Her hair, suggestively disheveled, is black and lustrous, rarely cut, undulating, her skin uniformly amber. Sorel introduces her in an offhand manner: "Odile, thirteen years and eight months old, but endowed with various precocious charms, will be a pretty plaything for you. Don't thank me. She is nothing but a little ha'penny whore, too happy to have been picked by your noble household before being completely spoiled by the inevitable vagaries of her harsh stock in trade."

45. Gigi seems mighty interested but would like further clarification: "A plaything of what kind?" Sorel's response is unambiguous: "Of the submissive object kind, for all uses." "So I shall be able to do with her anything I please, like with my childhood dolls? She won't be in a position to object if I slap her for no reason, lick her luscious mouth, or even bite her too hard? I'll dress her as it suits me, or else undress her completely to give her thrashings on her bottom, her belly, and her crotch? She'll let me do what I will even when I fondle the inside of her sex, gently or brutally? And to punish her, should it amuse me, I can hang her naked by one foot, the way I used to my cute dollies in the old days, whom I would whip in that position till their delicious howls could be heard..." "She is your toy," says the father, smiling, "so you can do whatever you want with her. But I am counting on your economic common sense not to risk definitively damaging such a precious trinket, like that pretty little girl made of moving plastic foam parts that you used to like so much, but whose legs you tore off in a temper one day because she refused to talk under torture."

46. The good little schoolgirl cracks a grin at this ultimately pleasurable recollection, contemplating her current prey, her eyelids lowered, with evident lust. Suddenly she orders, though with a certain sweetness, "Strip, little slut." With a prompt hand, Odile pops a single clasp and the dress of rags falls to her bare feet. Her minuscule lace underwear is now all that is shielding the adoles-

cent's proffered flesh. Gigi decides to turn it up a notch, "What are you waiting for, you idiot? Take off your disgusting panties!" The docile doll obeys, then wanting to appear composed, she carefully folds the sparse article of clothing to place it on a chair. She then executes, in silence, a series of slow twirls, so that her anatomy might be evaluated on the one side and the other, as well as in profile, while her arms wrap in soft curves around her undone hair, dark brown tinged with red. One can admire, on her small, round bottom, three affecting red scars, highly decorative, still moist and pearling in many spots, inflicted by the same slicing, for now imaginary, lash.

47. Her body is supple, undulating, and dancing. The tiniest of her movements proves graceful, her sweet kittenish face looks as though it is awaiting kisses, her shapely young charms require indiscreet hands, licentious caresses, and the cruel ardor of a real whip. As promised by the seller, her figure appears more developed than her age would indicate. A little less tall than Gigi, fortunately, and younger by nearly a year, she almost has a woman's body, freshly budding to be sure, but already with distinctly bountiful charms, hardly miniatures. Her pretty, well-rounded breasts, in particular, arouse the envy of her mistress, provisionally less well-endowed. This latter, meanwhile, glad to have such delectable gems at her mercy in the future, is rejoicing in advance at the prospect of making them pay for their imprudent advantage; for she appreciates, at its true worth, what it is to have a living doll, wanting in no respect, with which to entertain oneself without witnesses, as would all little girls, the world over, who perversely mistreat their favorite toy.

48. The thing, however, that most holds her voluptuous attention, is evidently the quite modest, but clear and well-defined triangle of fur, more russet than it is brown, covering the plump pubic cushion, and which, far from detracting the avid gaze, to the contrary, signals inside this scintillating jewel box a slit of pleasure no

doubt destined to become a favorite destination for games and vexations devised by a lover raised on erotic tales. Already she discerns, toward the base of the large lips, the pink mucus membrane of the slit shining with spontaneous saliva. Anxious to better dissimulate her emotion, Gigi asks Sorel with detachment: "Are her various orifices virgin?" But the man has a hard time keeping a straight face, given how ludicrous the supposition appears to him: "No, of course not, no more so in front than in the back," he answers, guffawing.

49. As though wanting to apologize, he adds: "Don't think me so chaste! Odile has been sleeping in my bed for what soon will be eighteen months, and putting aside my initial noble intentions, I didn't last three weeks so close to the forbidden fruit! In truth, I didn't know exactly what I was going to do with her when I culled this sullied pearl out of the stream, that is to say from the clandestine whorehouse, rather poorly run, where her parents prostituted her to any and all comers. Far from being poor, they had two other daughters, slightly older, less attractive, and hard to marry off without a dowry. To ensure their respectable marriages, they were selling, and at rather a high price, the childish allures of this young sacrificial lamb, with the exception that is, of her two traditional orifices, kept intact for a future husband. She was barely twelve and at the time was called "Dédette," her real name, Andrea, having been deemed ill-suited to the puerile uses being made of her, exceedingly limited, to boot, owing to the exorbitant hourly rates posted in the catalogue. Only her mouth, her hands, all her sleek nakedness, were on offer to those practitioners who, paradoxically, are aroused by virginities to which access is forbidden. The medieval prescription of double chastity, in its strictest materialization, no doubt contributed to their sacrilegious pleasures."

50. "The child's little lips were pierced, closely pressed together with a large, golden, coiled braid equipped with a lock whose keyhole, deliberately left in view, permitted the introduction of a mas-

sive, old-fashioned key, while at the same time firmly maintaining in place a curved stem that married the hollow curve of the crotch, penetrated the anus, and, inside her rectum, terminated in a pear. The manipulation of the unlocking mechanism, the exclusive domain of a few rare, trusty clients, and already sufficiently enticing, would subsequently authorize the selected few to touch her fragile vulva, her unperforated hymen, and her anal rosebud, once again closed shut. After which, they put everything back in its place and gave the key a couple of turns. The barbaric metal instrument caused the child to suffer, particularly when a clumsy client, looking for her clitoris, would bury an index finger in the narrowed slit, or unceremoniously spread her legs apart, or rub his prick between her ass cheeks. She cried often during these sessions, without ever putting up a fight.

51. "The tears of a very young sex object, decidedly, have their ardent champions, who at times deem them a requisite spice. For my own part, I was moved in a way that was more paternal by this admixture of tears, docile abandon, and contained sniffling. In a charitable flourish, to give her shelter, I bought the unhappy girl, paying in ready money for her overpriced double virginity with, nonetheless, marked on the invoice, 'private acquisition of all rights wanton or criminal, legal or outlawed.' Betrayed by her real parents, seduced by my libertarian ways, she began instantly to harbor a touching gratitude toward me. I left her injured charms alone, which I had relieved of their professional gear, keeping the instrument, however, for use as a nice punitive device in my harem of by and large naked pre-adolescent girls who usually served food at the bloody sacrificial feasts we would hold once in a while, and that you are quite familiar with yourselves. As with all who serve my pleasure, pubescent or not, Dédette was to be lashed regularly, on principal, as a reminder of her status as a helpless slave, that, none of these young women should forget. But, renamed Odile, under my purview, she was, in the beginning anyhow, relatively spared.

52. "Having become carefree and cheerful in mere days, seemingly in keeping with her child's nature, Odile found it great fun, after reciting her evening prayers on her knees, pulling off her nightgown swiftly, under the pretext of the excessive heat in my room, and slipping under the sheets to say good night to me up close. She would then kiss me on the mouth with sweet insistence, rubbing her intimate flesh against my pajamas. My protective arm was wrapped around her waist without any thought of wrongdoing, and my fingers wandered on her groins. Freed from the constraining duties of tariffed love, she revealed a teasing and sensual nature, unafraid, stripped of inhibitions. If I wished to interrupt these imprudent annoyances and to appease my increasing arousal, I would call for a service doll to come to bed in order to mistreat her, rape her, preferably a virgin resembling Odile whom I would barbarically deflower while another young servant was tortured in front of us, principally on the inside of her cunt, irrespective of whether it was brand new or already profaned. Their progressive suffering gradually staved my unquenched thirst. But Odile would instantly start sulking ostentatiously, as though these rivals were taking away what was hers, even when one of them was expiring by this or that delectable torture, the need for which she had made me feel.

53. "These amusing harem jealousies having lasted about two weeks, Odile, wanting to establish her rights and capabilities, was proving ever more resourceful. One night when my fingers lingered on her tight anal bud, while she was kissing me after her prayers, the girl, emboldened by my affectionate gesture suggested in a low voice that I should massage, with an emollient ointment, the conduit of her sphincter, which she claimed had been toughened by the pear of virtuous obstruction donned too frequently. After some minutes of appropriate friction, the sweet slut abruptly extended her body, opening herself up as far as possible so my fingers penetrated quite deeply. In a lover's whisper, she begged me to caress her most precious jewel as she guided my other hand to

her vulva, soaking around her erect clitoris, while the amorous movements of her rounded haunches, their slow rhythmic swell, could hardly be misapprehended. I slapped her several times and she began to cry, her pouting lips signaling bitter disappointment.

54. "I too, was disappointed and more seriously so, once more, by the craftiness of little girls, my decision was made ruthlessly: I summoned, for an altogether different purpose than that of servile concubines, three adolescent pleasure girls specializing in the punishment of their slave companions, one equipped with a vicious rigid-lashed whip, the other two with supple, sturdy thin ropes ending in flowing knots. Within seconds, Odile, now trembling in panicked terror, was placed prostrate on the bed, a black band obstructing her sight, her hands tied behind her back and her legs bound with ropes below the knees and at the ankles, yanked violently to each side to spread them to their maximum. The flagellating servant immediately began whipping the firm ass and its crack, well-displayed in this obscene pose, proffered to the sharp, slender leather lash that sliced its pretty culpable bud and its now firmly closed star. Very quickly blood pearled on her broken skin, here and there, this made the henchwoman laugh gleefully, having found it unfair that the little new girl should be cosseted daily, for no apparent reason, since her arrival. I was, myself, encouraging her to strike harder, slapping the distraught victim again, no longer giving a toss about this girl who would now be nothing more than an anonymous object of entertainment destined for the unbridled perversions of tormenting pedophiles never lacking in revolting cruelties. Announcing this, I brushed my erect penis over her face and between her panting lips, then against her backside, over her raw bottom, smeared in blood. And in a single stroke I buried myself inside her ass, copiously lubricated by the supposedly therapeutic massage, to savagely sodomize her while crushing the tip of her clitoris between my sharp nails. Her screams and moans blended harmoniously with the crystalline peals of the other three girls' laughter."

55. Odile, pulled to her feet and held firmly by Domenica, the girl administering the lashing, is contorting feebly in pain. She is losing blood in two charming bright red rivulets running down her thighs from the rips in her anus and from her clitoris, slightly truncated by its torn off tip. Sitting on the edge of the bed, Sorel contemplates her contentedly. He finds this tormented tender maiden very stirring, though she would now no doubt be headed for other punishments, customary here for little girls sentenced to death, no matter the scale of their supposed wrongdoing. He wants her flung to her knees at present, and grabbed her by her bleeding vulva as Domenica again lashes her bottom. Howling ever louder and sobbing, the blindfold still across her eyes, she begs for her master's forgiveness. "Quiet, bitch," he replies. To shut her up, he pulls her torso toward his voluminous cock that can no longer hold off the critical phase, and buries it inside her far-too-small mouth at the risk of suffocating the child. In the end he ejaculates his come in exceptional abundance on the lower half of Odile's choking face, which the thick opalescent liqueur covers as its meandering viscosity trickles down. Sorel orders the servants to take the young fallen princess to a preliminary punishment dungeon, chained so she can neither wash nor see to her bodily needs.

56. Domenica, Domi for short, then drags her prisoner along on a leash, forcing her to advance on her knees, which she is not allowed to bring any closer to one another. If she fails to move quickly enough, or looks like she might be bringing her thighs any closer together, one of the little girls assisting with punishments (younger than their leader, even) jabs her bottom with a porker's needle, ever delighted to add to the sufferings of a disgraced rival being led to her death. The distance is actually not far, the ceremonial nuptial chamber, situated as it used to be at the heart of these old abodes in the immediate proximity of the *fornax* and its adjacent facilities: those boudoirs of greater or lesser luxury for concubines, dungeons for condemned girls awaiting execu-

tion, rooms for entertainment, trials, libidinal feasts garnished with transgressions, there were also various premises for dressage, displays, tortures and other *deliciae*. The young captives occupying these were no longer, as they once were, Christian slaves, but whatever young females of *status variable* were available on the market.

57. Outside of the seven- to fourteen-year-old virgins delivered as war trophies, whose prolonged sexual torment and immolation by ancestral sadism (in the homes of rich individuals on public holidays, for instance) has been perpetuated through the ages, regulated by international accords, here one principally finds young women and adolescents sold at auction by their parents, a brother in debt, a disappointed husband, or sold by religious convents specializing in raising lost, abandoned little girls, as well as ones on the lam, quite often ravished by professional thieves. A final supply source that we must mention, increasingly significant: pretty (supposedly) convicted girls, sentenced to death by regular courts in their country of origin, Eastern Europe, the Middle East, South America, etc. said to have escaped, who have fallen into the hands of criminal multinationals and are ceded in the Occident at prices that defy all competition.

58. We must, in passing, note that these countries, exporters of living sinners to be made to perish in front of witnesses, very rarely punish men, and infinitely more often girls than mature, soon to be aging, women. Local sociologists attribute this disproportion to the great wisdom of gentlemen and their spouses. Progressives in our countries, on the other hand, suggest an altogether different analysis of the phenomenon, power in these countries belonging as it does to men and to their respectable spouses, highly vigilant in the surveillance of little girls, adolescents, and very young brides, who, if not watched over, easily stumble into the excesses of liberalism, witchcraft, revolutionary ideas, drugs, etc. We should point out a detail that seems important: these traditionalist societies

where the death penalty has not been abolished, even for minors, also retain the practice of some rather archaic modes of execution such as the stake, still so widespread at the turn of the century, be it anal or "natural," banned for obscenity, also still current are decapitations by axe of a kneeling victim, leaning gracefully into a block stained red with previously spilled blood that permanently adorns the central squares of small provincial towns, also practiced is the quartering by mounted horsemen astride fiery steeds, supplanted today in the interest of greater control over the progressive tearing apart of limbs, by four enormous winches with manual transmission, often found in private homes.

59. Otherwise, little has evolved. Meanwhile, the victims, for understandable reasons of decency, were submitted for public viewing wearing a billowing penitent's robe of thick cloth with a great hood. But this gave rise to too many fraudulent arrangements and easy substitutions such as the dismemberment of a cadaver or a rag doll even. Justice today requires that guilty girls walk to punishment entirely naked and submit without a sheath to the meticulous enactment of their sentence. Transgressions are now of a different order. Most henchmen, aroused by the feminine charms exposed for all to see (and the more or less necessary manipulations by the executioners), further affected by the winsome postures deriving from the verdict, have obtained from their professional unions the right to exclusive fondling and to multiple rapes of the powerless prey whose hands remain shackled, before and during the torture that they naturally prolong beyond what was intended, with pauses and resumptions, fast transforming the edifying *mise en scène* of judicial remedy into a voluptuous torture session, subsequently reported in the popular press in long, erotic accounts illustrated with numerous suggestive photographs.

60. Influential journalists have even issued calls at the highest levels for the reinstatement of the spectacularly dissuasive practices of olden-days capital punishments. Among these, one method in

particular concerns adultery, passive sodomy, lesbianism, masturbatory pleasures, and all forms of female (hence diabolic) depravity, whether in adult women or girls. Any female suspected of these proclivities, submitted to interrogation per the rigorous medieval protocol, confessed, without the least difficulty, to her wrongdoing, intended or accomplished, her established depravity, her lascivious conduct, and the indecent thoughts that dwelled in her permanently. Condemned to death in every case, as a matter of principle, she was paraded naked in the public square and made, on her knees, to face those that had hastened to gather to hear her confess to her innumerable crimes, punctuated by incisive lashings given by three statutory henchmen.

61. Next, they would crucify her upside down, her young body, so far fairly unscathed, drawn between two vertical poles about a meter apart, to which she was attached with enormous wrought-iron nails hammered deep into her ankles, and below, through her palms. It was possible then, leisurely, to exorcise her sex thoroughly, with the appropriate tools: double-bladed hunting knives, phalluses trimmed with spikes, sharp, long-toothed saws, red hot pincers, etc. After consecutive sessions of this expiatory ritual, she was left to die a natural death, her spasms revived occasionally to affirm their breadth and intensity, with the legendary flaming tar pitch poured on her pubis and around it, which completed, by its glow in the falling night, the profoundly religious character of the ceremony.

62. Although very much in vogue and having given rise to infinite versions, depending on the size, age, and physical traits of the victim (a girl child who was too little would first have her legs pulled apart into splits and beyond, in order to successfully nail her ankles to the two posts; with a child-woman, breastfeeding the fruit of sin, her breasts were ripped off first; a tall, vigorous girl had her knees shattered with a chisel to soften the angularity of her startled jolts of pain, and so forth), this edifying punishment

was excluded from the code under the absurd pretext that crucified girls took too long to die. Whereas, the only thing the unanimous crowds demanded was that a thick cushion be placed under the victim's neck to avoid cerebral accidents due to the afflux of congestive blood, allowing several more hours for the contemplation of the splendid, suffering contortions these hussies deserved.

63. Politicians, on the other hand, would have liked to abolish all these scandalous displays, which, nonetheless, attracted a great many wealthy tourists. But the only practical solution devised, with the help of traffickers, was to sell the most delectable of the condemned of all ages in this prosperous Occident where debauchery flourishes. Here too, unfortunately, there was a hitch. The market having turned profitable, criminals began to specialize in the fabrication of fake guilty girls, identifying pretty defenseless young things, easy to put on trial and convict without the slightest evidence. It must be pointed out in this regard that if a girl child not yet six should receive the death penalty, she is immediately exonerated. The young mother, deemed responsible, will be tortured in her stead. In cases of exportation, to dispose of the little girl with whom no one knows what to do, she is left as a bonus for the foreign buyer, who will have to make them both disappear, an example of which we shall soon see.

64. Odile, led by her juvenile guards who are given to giggling, finally arrives at her dungeon. When Domi, their accredited leader, opens its unlocked door, she immediately sees that this cell, reserved, like the ones next to it, for those awaiting death, is already occupied, though not for long it would seem. Where orders received are concerned, however, the loyal enforcer is not one to question them. The two little girls accompanying her, although they have by now witnessed numerous barbaric tableaux in this abode that is vowed to amorous excess, cannot suppress a shudder of horror. The straw serving as a bed is awash in the blood of two freshly sacrificed victims, a very young mother, her breasts swollen

with milk, and a cherub of about eighteen months, no doubt her daughter, bled to death after horrendous tortures. Domi, a torturer in training for the last few months, and new expert in oriental cruelties favored by the master, for her part, experiences a sort of aesthetic respect for this tableau.

65. The breastfeeding mother, who must be barely fifteen, is straddling a tree cutters' saw, whose long steel teeth have lacerated her pubis deeply. Her torso is held in place vertically by two chains pulled obliquely, each equipped with a butcher's hook piercing the palms of her hands. Her legs are spread very wide, but pulled less widely apart than her arms, arranged more loosely using identical hooks that pierce her ankles so her greater movements in the course of the torture should further tear her vulva, her inner groin, and the jointure of her ass… To this end, her armpits, the tips of her breasts and their areolas, the crux of her groins, her navel, her anus have been burned by red hot irons, and the fur of her blond pussy scalped. Only then, have great gashes been made in her bottom, breasts, and thighs, carefully, so as not to cut into any large arteries, and her wounds doused in anti-coagulating alcohol.

66. Her baby has been left still suckling at the maternal breast, which never fails to inflame the criminal lust of practitioners. One can tell already that it's a girl, by her sweet, pretty, golden curls and precociously sexy expressions. Widened by the blade of a knife, in front of her still very much living mother, she has been raped on both sides multiple times, before being impaled on a far-too-large phallus (the tiles of the dungeon, under the straw, are equipped with fixtures designed for adapting such accessories) in order to also burn her flesh with the red hot irons that are alternately addressing her wet-nurse's tits. The latter, deflowered three years prior by an older brother while in her twelfth year, soon found herself pubescent, then pregnant. Denounced by her rapist who, after excessive use, tired of her, she found herself condemned for provoca-

tive immodesty, forbidden games, fornication, prolonged incest, procreation outside marriage, concealment of a baby, etc. Her charms undiminished, quite the contrary, she was sold without the slightest difficulty, for exportation.

67. Odile meanwhile, whose eyes are still blindfolded and whose hands remain tied behind her back, has yet to perceive her cellmate. Her custodians have chained her up, as per Sorel's instructions, right next to the tortured, innocent girl. Hung by her feet to the arches, her legs spread wide, only her head and shoulders rest on the straw-covered floor. Humbly she asks to pee. Without answering, Domi removes the band from her eyes and shows her the state of her neighbor, so she might grasp the destiny that awaits her. Odile, petrified, murmurs, "Is she dead?" "Not quite, as you can see," assures Domi, violently lashing the young mother's belly with the whip, which merely provokes a delayed, feeble shuddering. To make her appreciate the difference, the merciless guard, in all her child's cruelty, strikes Odile's belly in the same way, this latter, now at the height of panic, again implores to at least be allowed to relieve her pressing need for urination.

68. Her tormentor, laughing, tells her there's nothing to stop her, and the slicing lash, this time, lands on her parted sex, all the more painful for having been lightly mutilated by Sorel. As the too-long-contained urine gushes, blushing lightly with the blood from her clitoris, Domi, on cloud nine, delivers repeated lashes to the source of this spring, which grows progressively redder, inundating all of the sleek body displayed upside down. The two little girls clap gleefully. Before their mistress has even completed her punishment, following suit, they too pee, first the one, then the other, on the abject face where Sorel's sperm is just beginning to dry. Now soiled, down to her hair and eyes, Odile is left to the terrifying silence of the dungeon, whose lights have just been turned off.

69. Here, then, is the same Odile, but a year and a half later. She is entirely naked again, this time in front of Gigi, who is admiring her pretty body decorated with artfully painted lash marks on her breasts, pubis, buttocks, all of which charms are markedly more developed than they were in the preceding paragraphs. So Sorel recounts the start of her training with perfect nonchalance, as if the girl brought as a gift were not standing there, perfectly visible, smiling, immobile, as absent as though she belonged to another world, no blindfolds covering her pretty, vacant eyes. Gigi has received the answer to her naïve question: no, the doll of flesh is no longer in any way a virgin, which is preferable actually, declares the good little schoolgirl, realizing, gradually, the delicacy of her own position in this convoluted affair.

70. Unexpectedly involved in an unpredictable and multipolar intrigue, she must, from this initial contact, demonstrate her confidence, maturity, as well as her gift for tyranny and inexplicable capriciousness, contrary to her upbringing, and that, up till now at least, would hardly have seemed in her nature. From here on, if she wants to maintain relative control over events, she must show not the tenderness she feels for her new companion, but a domineering, intransigent rigor, albeit make-believe. A few flourishes of gratuitous cruelty would even be advisable. And she senses, in this brand new challenge, a particular phase of her schooling, no doubt thoughtfully devised by her father's tutelary, paternal authority. Overcoming her instinctive timidity, she complies with the necessary exigency of touching this all too perfect Odile, not with a gentle caress, but as one might touch a freak at a fair, and this even, she does in as outrageous a manner as possible, making it clear in this way that she is officially taking possession of what henceforth belongs to her by rights.

71. Seated, since the visitors arrived, on the shiny wicker garden chair, she barks, without faltering: "Over here, on your knees, and spread your thighs so I can see if your russet pussy suits me."

The schoolgirl, on this occasion, is able to gauge the value of the erotic readings prescribed by her father, and of the apprenticeship they have afforded her in comparable situations. But she feels as though she's walking a fine line. By a stroke of luck, the doll obeys instantly. She even adds a flourish that often perfects the pose, lifting her arms, elbows half bent, to frame her suddenly fearful tortured child's face, which actually suits her marvelously. As she has certainly been taught to do, she holds her hands quite far on either side of her face so as not to appear to want to protect herself: this is not a gesture of defense, but the unconditional surrender of a consenting victim. Forbidding herself from giving in to an impulsive desire to kiss her passionately, Gigi, with a sure right hand, lifts Odile's chin and gives her a hard slap, plain and loud.

72. Then her hand moves down to a breast, which she fondles for a moment, somewhat brutally, to feel its soft firmness before pinching its little tip brutally, so hard that a jolt traverses the girl's torso, whose mouth opens in response to the unforeseen (not to mention unforeseeable) pain, without changing her pose, hallowed by centuries of voluptuous submission. Gigi strikes her once more, a slap so violent on each cheek that her widened green eyes blur with silent tears. But, very swiftly, the punishing hand descends, this time to her belly, and thrusts, not without savagery, three nimble fingers inside her vulva. A new clenching makes the child, gripped by fear, contort further, as tears stream down her face, reddened by the slaps.

73. Gigi, meanwhile, encouraged for having felt under her aggressive fingers, on penetration, the fragile mucous membrane completely soaked, begins to masturbate her aroused clitoris, whose impatience is evident, alternating slow delicacies with more applied vigor, soon implementing this blend using both her hands, as she has been doing on herself for some time in her attempts at masturbating. Odile, relieved of her anguish by this felicitous

change, relaxes immediately, moans a little, arches her back to better proffer her sex to her mistress's expert phalanges. She promptly shows unequivocal signs of pleasure. Sorel remarks to his friend that the girl, like many older ones, is quickly aroused by preliminary mistreatment, constrained nudity, shameful poses, humiliating language, slaps, various ropes and chains, the simulacra of rape, etc. So, most gentlemen whip their young spouses before making love to them. It is habitually believed that the male's atavistic goal is the fulfillment of his own appetites. But, in many instances, it is the little female in heat that this excites the most.

74. They had not spoken very audibly but could Gigi's sharp ears, perhaps, have picked up wisps of their sentences? In between the sighs and amorous moans of her at last conquered doll, she says to the two men, their respective chaperones: "I want this impudent slut to be whipped in order to put an end to these inopportune demonstrations. She must, what's more, be punished for not having taken her panties off straight away, forcing me to repeat my order for her to strip naked." Sorel stands up with a smile of approbation. He is already holding in his hand, ready to deploy, a thin crop of stiff leather, the extension of a very short ivory handle that ends in a turgescent phallic gland, crystal studded, an ostensible torture dildo. Standing behind his pupil, he orders: "Apologize!" "Forgive me, Mistress," implores the terrorized Odile, whose sex Gigi now grabs with all the savage force of which she is capable, three fingers bury themselves deep inside, while her palm folds over the perfumed russet fur doused in vaginal liquid, without warning she pinches one of its large lips in a way that immobilizes the sweet trembling ass on to which falls the first stroke in a dry snap. Odile cries out, frantic, overcome, but assisted by the iron hand whose sharp nails risk cutting into her vulva, she manages to maintain her pose.

75. "Apologize, you little, ill-bred slut!" repeats Sorel. In the same pretty, fruity, juvenile, supplicating voice, which had not been

heard since the opening of the gift box, the adolescent repeats, trembling: "Forgive me, Mistress …" And straight away a second lash, still more violent, strikes the round of her captive bottom. The same cry of distress, further prolonged, resounds under the arcades, while the unjustly punished child bursts into sobs. Under the strain of the commotion, she seems about to faint… From her historic readings, Gigi has retained that the rapid alternating of sexual gratification and delicate, very painful injuries was a torture relegated by an emperor of the Tang dynasty for his new concubines whose nocturnal services he had not found satisfactory. They would die of it after some hours, without their charms having been disfigured, adorned simply with multiple burns, gashes on which blood beaded, and other excisions that, on the contrary, underscored their beauty. If the nobleman wearied of seeing them expire slowly, he would have them devoured alive by his dogs, nailed to the ground so the beasts could begin their meal unhurriedly, starting with the pubis and inner groin, their favorite morsels, together with the milk-swollen breasts of young mothers.

76. Odile, for her part, is already so traumatized that she reveals her utter disarray by pitiful weeping. She lowers her arms and timidly paws at the cruel hand imprisoning her poor little pussy in a raptor's clutch. She stammers while snuffling large tears "I'm sorry, Mistress, I'm sorry…" When the third lash of the whip falls, she collapses in on herself with a howl, then kisses the bare feet of Gigi, who has finally released her. Rather pleased with the results that have surpassed all her expectations, the latter, with a casual toe, offhandedly musses the locks of the slave lying on her belly traversed by spasms that make her shake feebly, conquered twice over and good only for throwing to the sadistic emperor's dogs. Then again, the three bright red lines crisscrossing the two delicately-shaped, dimpled globes, without having flayed the sleek skin, make her tender rump resplendent with a dazzle as sensual as it is decorative, infinitely more affecting than the fake painted

lash marks. The mistress bends over them to lightly graze the art with a possessive index finger, acknowledging her power to inflict more pain should it amuse her. The skin, in the most affected spots, has turned so sensitive that the delectable little buttocks are overrun by shivers.

77. Gigi, justifiably, thinks that she has won this difficult round. Odile, on the other hand, in her humiliating defeat, looks nothing like a loser: she instinctively senses that the licentious interest accorded her future victim by the mistress from the outset has just been transformed into true enchantment in what, it turns out, is their first carnal union ... This is when the storm erupts: an immense bolt of lightning first, dazzling even in broad daylight, followed a few seconds later by a long, very long, roll of thunder. And the rain starts to fall, dense and heavy, sounding like a cataract. Grateful to the sky gods for these baptismal waters, a present to dissolve the highly charged atmosphere that was beginning to be oppressive for all three couples (the father and his too-fondly loved daughter, the second man and his new adolescent mistress, the two girls beginning their honeymoon) Gigi, spontaneously, throws off her *djellaba*, raises the wounded doll, and drags her under the munificent shower.

78. Laughing like mad coots, they hop together into the fountain, whose water only reaches their knees, and start to dance naked, holding hands, or hugging to rub against each other, kissing, licking, fondling each other's bellies and breasts, as though in a mutual grooming session under the tropical deluge blessing their union and cooling Odile's stinging bottom where the lash marks stand out better, now that the rain has washed off their watercolor simulacra. Gigi compliments her on her durable stigmata, as well as on the adroit precision displayed by her lover and owner. "Never has he whipped me this hard before," confides the girl in her ear, forgetting the already distant episode of the punishment dungeon. "I thought I was going to die of the stinging burning

that sliced through me." "I know. I was inside you, feeling each stroke in the soft inside of your pussy, which was palpitating with these delicious, convulsive shudders. You were fainting under my astounded hand." The rain having stopped as abruptly as it had come, the two children take a few steps, hand in hand, intentionally splattering spectacular sprays of water in a squealing contest, squirting plumes as far as the enigmatic statue of white stone, whose figures are the same size as them. Odile holds her fingers under the young pisser's sprinkle while Gigi whispers dirty secrets to her in a low voice, as little girls do when alone.

79. "If that isn't a love match made under auspicious stars…" says Sorel (delighted by the success his gift has garnered). The father watches the two adolescents, one as ravishing as the other, playing with the melodious tinkling of their younger sister in marble. He is thinking that two pretty, naked girls fooling around add up to much more than twice a single, pretty girl. It's more as though the unique sexual object were multiplied by four. "Four pupils in my school," he finds himself imagining… "Four tender dolls in my bed…" But coming back to reality, slightly melancholy from thinking of the future, he says: "If Gigi marries Odile, she will leave me to sleep alone. I should go back with you to the house of pleasure where we met. You'll help me choose a pleasure slave there along the same lines as yours… Thirteen years old, O Romeo, the same age as Juliet…"

80. "I've told you before that was where, long ago, I met Violetta, Gigi's mother. She was barely eleven and a virgin everywhere. After having undressed, kissed, fondled her in hardly a decent manner, but not too insistently, and placing her in all sorts of postures that she found very amusing, especially the most indecent ones, and having asked her a thousand questions in order to judge her intellectual faculties, I decided to buy her from her parents for my self alone, whereas they were thinking of selling her by the day. They were not poor, far from it, and so they wanted a con-

siderable sum for her, advised by an attorney, well-known in this somewhat specialized market. The little girl was exquisite, sensually very promising, her at once thoughtful and cheerful nature suited me. I paid, without arguing, the asking price, 'for all uses,' which implies the inclusion of criminal ones, a notation rarely made in contract letters. Little Violetta was enchanted. This house she was entering as a luxury toy seemed much prettier than hers, with more servants, bigger grounds, a pool, etc. And my bachelor's conjugal quarters were sumptuous. She did not make a fuss at all about sleeping in my arms without panties or a nightie. The bathroom appeared so marvelous to her that she agreed beforehand to prolong, under my gaze, her most intimate toilette in there, which she did gracefully, coming over and kissing me to apologize whenever she felt too ashamed.

81. "A handsome young man, tall and vigorous, like in a fairy tale, I was rich, sophisticated, funny, original, and extremely kind to her (to start with, anyhow) whereas her brute of a father used to beat her without even enjoying it, which is horribly vexing for a pretty girl, whatever her age. I, very quickly, taught her to use her mouth, which was agile and fleshy, and with which I contented myself for several months, all the more easily since, very curious regarding matters sexual, my Violetta was avid to learn all that would turn her into an accomplished mistress. And she swallowed sperm without showing the slightest hint of aversion, only the grimaces of a child who is full, sometimes, when the thickness of the discharge in the back of her throat was too abundant. I was surprised by her natural gifts, pleased with her daily progress, seduced by her intelligence, which was precocious and devoid of taboos.

82. "Among the young servants of my household, there was a tall sixteen-year-old girl called Zerline, blond, shapely, with a carefree temperament, who had long since met the wolf. She would willingly come to my bed and eagerly submit to all my whims, for

which, by the way, I remunerated her generously. Violetta, my darling virgin in training, never one to forego an opportunity for learning, had immediately insisted on staying with us during our libertine frolics, and she was fascinated by the variety of obscene positions in which one can penetrate either of the two orifices presented by a pretty and obliging rump. Naked herself too, the little girl would strive to reproduce the contortions, back bends, splits, and excessive dislocations, a fine exercise in stretching. She was, moreover, allowed to touch her model, to smell her, to taste her secret savor. Humiliation and punishment were of even greater interest to her.

83. "Wishing to put this proclivity to the test, I had, through a very serious agency, with whom I ran no risks of running into trouble, hired a debutante prostitute who had, apparently, just committed a grave error and therefore had to be punished with all the customary cruelty of the profession, if only to set an example. By way of thanks for a service rendered to the sub-mistress, this latter had asked me to administer the punishment foreseen to Lily. On paper, the girl was eighteen years old, but the vacant prettiness of her naïve face made her seem much younger (which she probably was). Her skin was exceedingly soft to the touch, her figure, in bloom, lacked any thickness, was supple and sensitive. I kept her locked in a dungeon of delight (one of five *deliciae* my Roman home could boast) and I planned to make her suffer there for several days for the pleasure and education of my little fiancée.

84. "When she saw her for the first time, Lily was already positioned for the execution of the sentence: her plump cunt was to be lashed over and over. So her legs were up, pulled apart almost in the splits. Blood flowed from the multiple cuts of the whip on her inner groin, bright red and rather runny thanks to the anti-coagulating agent that was administered from time to time. The guilty girl (was she really, and of what, precisely?) was weeping and moaning with childish grace. Dazzled by the spectacle,

Violetta kissed me fervently to thank me for the sumptuous gift. Then she asked would it not be better to rip off the girl's thick russet muff, which had nothing aesthetically pleasing about it and in fact, presented an inconvenience to the lashes that would better sear the fragile flesh of a hairless pussy and might even be able enter the slit, disjointed by the splits. I told her the simplest thing would be to burn off the muff with a candle, and suggested she herself do it.

85. "The condemned girl, who could hear our conversation, struggled fruitlessly in her chains, sobbing ever harder and begging in tones of understandable terror. But her position was too tempting and her desperate imploring only further aroused the desire of her tormentors. After pouring pure alcohol between her thighs, which already made her howl, my diligent little girl promptly moved the flame to the base of the triangle (that is to say to the top of her muff had it been right side up). A magnificent blue gleam, turned yellow and red as it spread to the top, the flame crackling amid the brush and the howls of the torture victim. Violetta poured on more alcohol to keep the flames going, then moved the candle closer again, allowing a few drop of burning wax to drip onto the brazier. Once the hair removal was deemed satisfactory the punished young whore appeared so enfeebled that she had to be made to drink a reviving tonic dripped in between her parted lips, her head and neck resting on the ground. Next my thin crop of stiff leather landed on her crotch making various patterns. Her skin, turned fragile by the flames that had licked her pubis, her vulva and inner thighs immediately streamed with blood. I continued striking her until she fainted for good, while Violetta, prostrate, was kissing her passionately on the mouth and caressing her breasts.

86. "A girl whom one has destined for a brilliant career, as a legitimate wife or as a ceremonial courtesan, must appreciate great music, even if, personally, she plays no other instrument than her

body. Violetta's parents had given her, very early on, a marked taste for classical opera, which simultaneously satisfied her sensuality, her opulent penchants, and her exhibitionism. For my part, each season, I subscribed and rented a box, where I had the leisure of showing off my favorites, whatever their age, and at the same time as finding myself alone with them. During a magnificent staging of *Butterfly*, my budding fiancée was kneeling against the balustrade leaning toward the stage, her elbows on the velvet padding. I fondled her firmly under her wide, pleated, schoolgirl skirt where the flesh was like silk. She let me do as I wished without pulling away. Then, looking at me with huge, trusting eyes, as my fingers worked their way further in, she smiled and without saying a word, she removed her panties, taking up her position again afterwards, but spreading her thighs much wider apart.

87. "I fondled, for over an hour, with both hands, her anal bud and her clitoris, using an aphrodisiac ointment that I had brought along. She was so wet in front that her mucus was dripping on to my fingers. And she would shift her bottom from time to time, arching as though seeking to better accommodate me on her posterior side as well, my index and middle fingers, burying themselves gradually in the too-narrow channel, massaging the inside of which did not appear to displease her. The curtain having come down on stage, I asked if my indiscretion had not interfered with her enjoyment of this masterpiece of lyrical art. With great gravity, she replied no, on the contrary, it was very appropriate to Puccini's sentimentalism. With respect, she seized my left hand, the one that was entirely impregnated with her, to inhale it for a moment, before placing it under my nose, 'Don't you think?' she murmured looking her most innocent.

88. "For her twelfth birthday, I gave a great banquet in her honor where wine, drugs, and alcohol favored general licentiousness consisting of rapes and the habitual tortures inflicted on little girls and other comely young people providing services, the precious

Zerline, the servant mistress who had achieved the rank of sultane, was employed on this occasion as an assistant torturer. After dessert and liqueurs, Violetta suddenly asked, as a birthday gift, that Zerline should come and kneel at her feet, entirely naked, with her hands tied behind her back to lick her quim (the pretty old-fashioned word that she always used to refer to her vulva) while I myself lashed the prostrated sultane's bottom with a particularly painful whip. The sweet servant declared her willingness to adopt this rather classic pose, but wanted to be paid quite dearly, on top of her servant's wages apparently, and her fee as a whore. To sell herself for money, constituted for her, a kind of sexual stimulant, even when she made love for pleasure. I gave her the significant sum we agreed upon.

89. "But when she was securely bound to the floor by her ankles, and her knees spread, her arms chained together above her waist, and Violetta's hands firmly held her by her blond, disheveled curls, so as to crush her mouth against her already rather moist quim, I resolved, displeased with her haggling, to strike my mistress quite cruelly so as to make her cry out in pain. 'Lick it better, you clumsy slut!' said the little girl. I applied two severe lashes, back to back, to Zerline's bottom, which improved her sucking on the clitoris, and buried the whip's alarmingly large handle inside her anus. She protested feebly, her lips drowning in the folds of the vulva. And promptly received three supplementary strokes, more brutal still. Next, I masturbated her injured bud extensively with the protuberant humped handle, which increasingly tore into her as she applied herself, whimpering bitterly, to grazing her young rival's pussy.

90. "Violetta having raised her head to slap her three consecutive times, Zerline begged for my clemency for the tiny tabernacle where I had always taken such marked pleasure discharging my spunk. I ordered her to shut up and whipped her till she broke down in tears. I then sodomized her properly, my cock sliding in

the blood spread by the multiple small wounds, causing her new pain instead of the lively anal orgasms she habitually experienced. Violetta, triumphant, was slapping her ever harder and pinching the tips of her breasts between her nails, eliciting new howls, and making those marvelous adolescent charms that she had so coveted bleed.

91. "When I put an end to the (no doubt unjust) torture of the humiliated sultane sapped of her strength, and had placed a tiny complicit kiss on her lips which she returned lovingly, the brave girl dared to give me a warning: 'Beware, my Master, of this child. She loves you and she is jealous. If you let her do as she will, you will not have another moment of peace. I deserved the lashing, maybe, that's for you to decide, and even the barbaric dildo. But your spoilt child needs it more than I do.' This was the night that without any explanations, I had the precocious, ambitious and possessive little girl thrown onto the straw of a dungeon of degradation, where she remained captive for several weeks before returning to favor. Zerline, furthermore, was quite useful to me in my Violetta's cruel dressing down."

92. While our two gentlemen, sheltered from the downpour under the arcades, were thus evoking the romantic past one of them had shared with the girl child that was Gigi's mother, this latter had returned to the middle of the shallow pool with Odile, the young slave belonging to the other man. She was kneeling in the water in front of her sweet friend to kiss her sleek, blond pussy, while holding her bottom in her raised hands, and soon she was licking the slit, attempting to introduce her tongue inside. In a low voice she said "You are wet, too." "No I'm not," Gigi protested, "it's just the storm." In an even more confidential tone, Odile rejected this untruth: "That's not rain I'm tasting, it's the delicious taste of you!" And she licks more insistently having succeeded in burying the tip of her tongue between the glistening lips. Gigi strives to insert some severity in her reprimand: "Whether it's wet

or not, one does not use familiar terms with one's mistress! Stay where you are, I am going to punish you." The slave shuts her eyes and offers her sweet face up to the forthcoming slap. But, here is Gigi, taking her head in her hands and placing it between her thighs. When Odile feels the liquid streaming on her raised face at first she thinks the storm has started again. But no, it's warm and scented. The mistress is urinating steadily, with intense pleasure, on the face of her love doll, who opens her mouth to drink a bit of the punishment running past her lips and onto her tongue.

93. A treaty of subjection thus closed by mutual consent, the problem of bedrooms obviously arises: where would Odile sleep? Concerning Sorel, the matter had been settled some months earlier: he was to undertake, as early as the following night, a long professional trip where he would be in the company of foreign colleagues who would have been surprised, shocked even, by the presence in his luggage of so scandalously underage a beloved, who moreover, did not even have a passport! Odile, for her part, who liked physical contact with males and readily tolerated their domination, but emotionally preferred the ambiguous *eros* of young ladies, would have loved to sleep with Gigi. But the latter was categoric: nothing was to change in the household. Sleeping with dolls was something she had outgrown! And a mistress does not share a bedroom with sex slaves. She, therefore, would continue to spend her nights, most of the time entirely naked, in the arms of her educator, who found this all the less inconvenient as he was, moreover, thinking of welcoming into the vast paternal bed the pretty hired objects whose charms, to date, he had been enjoying in various ways at the brothel frequented by Sorel.

94. Odile would therefore be set up in one of the *deliciae* of which there has already been mention, seldom used here for some time, both love chambers, as perfectly suited to vice, as they are to rest and grooming, and torture dungeons decked out with rings, hooks, pulleys, and winches. As the mistress wishes to forbid her

little private whore any solitary masturbations generated by such an evocative décor, she would stop by each evening to bid this new boarder good night after making love to her (tenderly or savagely) and would then lock, not only the exterior door, but also the padlock to the shackles binding her hands behind her back. Partial to symbols, she thinks she might even chain her to the bed by one foot, to materialize both her status as prisoner and as a sweet ragdoll for debauchery. In the guise of compensation for this nocturnal chastity, the adolescent will be obliged, exposed naked in front of her masters, in chains that, nonetheless, leave her hands free, to publicly caress her own anus and clitoris, in particular in the course of the sado-licentious reading sessions, or to appear as a libertine living statue at dinners held for friends.

95. This chamber of sexual servitude assigned to Odile, the most beautiful of the cells equipped with multiple delights in the vast house, has walls covered not with paintings on canvas, but with six or seven images representing tortured girls. These are, for the most part, excellent photographic prints, under glass, in old-fashioned gilded stucco frames. Gigi thinks she has never before entered this kind of room, whose existence she had merely suspected. She promptly notes that the various photographs in question were taken on the premises: the same room layout, easily recognizable, the same mahogany Empire-style furniture, with pseudo-Egyptian bronzes, the same torture accessories. The only notable difference is constituted by the artworks on the walls, which were, at the time, eighteenth-century engravings. And also by the great mirrors in which to look at oneself, now installed on the ceiling. In place of the glass of a pier glass, a color photograph of the same dimensions has been substituted, in which we see a nymph, slender and well-turned, hanging upside down over the bed, her long legs pulled in opposite directions toward the vaulted ceiling by oblique chains binding her ankles. Her thighs are spread to the extreme and, totally naked, she is proffering her sex, conveniently, to the invisible tormentor.

96. Gigi lingers with acute interest on the details of her position, pointing out to Odile the admirable contraption upon which this latter is highly likely to find herself strung should she merit such punishment... on the day, that is, when her mistress might feel the wish to subject her to it. She shows her that the chains hanging over the bed are still in place, that the winch operating them is in perfect order (the handle, indeed, sets into motion, without the least difficulty, the well-oiled machinery) and that the wide, thickly padded leather cuffs in which they end are, decidedly, the same ones confining the ankles of the photographed girl. Her shoulders rest on an overstuffed cushion, her head hanging backward. Her lips are parted as if she were crying out feebly. Abundant blond hair surrounds her face on pale blue sheets. Her hands, unseen, are manifestly chained behind her back. Her eyes are covered by a black band. A wide trickle of bright red blood has run across her belly from her pubic slit to her already well-formed breasts. The inside of her thighs is crosshatched with dark carmine lines that are definitely real lash marks.

97. When Gigi returns to her father she asks him who this pretty person is. Had he known her, disciplined her himself? He hesitates, barely, before answering her, having no doubt expected this sort of question. "That's your mom, the splendid Violetta, when she was fifteen years old, that is to say right after our marriage." "And the other photos hanging in the room?" "Those are her too, at different periods of our life together. The dates are inscribed on the back in her own hand. In the oldest one, where she can be seen crying as she straddles a trestle whose sharp ridge is spreading the lips of her sex, she is only twelve years and a few months old. In the last one, the one where she is kneeling, impaled by her cunt on a huge brass phallus that is distending her vulva, her magnificent breasts awash in blood, lacerated by the whip, she must be eighteen, in other words, it's taken two years after you were born." "Why is she always bound?" "She truly loved me to whip her. To be pinned down for these voluptuous punishments, in very

coercive chains, lacerating ones even, relieved her conscience. It dispelled her feelings of guilt." Gigi has the impression that before her, another world has suddenly opened up in which her mother's mysterious disappearance has acquired an altogether new meaning. After intense reflection, she ends up saying, hiding her emotion: "I understand her."

98. The evening's dinner, served in the grand dining room, had been very lively, like a dream at once solemn and joyous. In the afternoon, under the pretext of inspecting Odile's astonishing prostitute's wardrobe and sub-wardrobe, Gigi had dallied into her lascivious lair. Further fascinated by the luxurious sado-erotic photographs ever since learning the name of the disquieting victim, she decided abruptly, in homage to this mythic, essentially unknown mother, to experiment by adopting the humiliating and obscene poses in which the machinery showed her over the bed. So, Odile tied her arms behind her back, higher than her waist so as to properly display her bottom, and adjusted the wide black leather cuffs at her ankles, then she placed the black band across her eyes. The manual winch was so smooth to operate that the upside-down body of the sacrificial doll rose slowly toward the vaulted ceilings of the dungeon, until it stopped naturally in the exact position admired in the photograph, her legs spread in a very wide V, the downy nest of her blond sex proffered to the mercy of red hot pokers, scalpels, and pincers.

99. Odile subjected her fake victim's bottom to a few dry snaps of the whip, which she handled with all the vigor required of her by Gigi, who was starting to moan. Her servant-tormentor kissed her pussy tenderly to console her. Next, five or six less insistent lashes were applied to the fragile dimple of each thigh. And Gigi, gradually losing control, allowed her rattling in pain to grow louder. The servant, then, going beyond the orders received, took advantage of the band blinding her mistress to set the whip down on the sheets, opening the adored vulva soaked in its secretions with

both her hands, licking it a little for her own pleasure, then taking the already swollen clitoris in between her teeth, squeezing just enough, and grazing its hardened bulb with the tip of her tongue. The dainty moans and whimpers of the supposed victim immediately change in nature and soon in their intensity, quickly reaching indecency. When Odile, further, stuffed two lubricant-imbued fingers inside the instantly receptive anus she started to cry out so loudly in pleasure that she would have roused the entire household were it not that the premises of the *deliciae* were devised precisely for stifling the howls of suffering of captives being tortured to death.

100. Driven mad by her partner's competencies, the good little girl appeared capable of having an indefinite number of orgasms in successive, ever closer waves. But she was traversed by such violent spasms that the wary servant feared she might seriously injure her ankles, in spite of the cushioned shield of the cuffs, submitted as they were to excessive shaking. In the ardent whisper of a hopeless love she intoned: "You are a dirty little bitch. And I'm going to have to watch you so you don't do anything stupid." By switching on the reverse command on the mechanical system, set in motion this time simply by the body weight, she began releasing Gigi, who felt as though she were floating weightlessly, as the protective voice changed its tenor, "Madam must not forget that she is presiding at her father's grand dinner tonight. If Madam permits, we shall now proceed to groom her."

101. Weakened by the long nervous tension and the successive orgasms, Gigi finds it practical to submit to the proposed care without even managing its administration. Odile's bathroom lacks the luxury of the professor's, nevertheless, it offers all the necessary comforts. Forgetting the imperatives of social hierarchy, the young mistress allows herself to be handled like a child. One might think she were dreaming that her servant is seating her softly on the walnut toilet seat to pee; and Odile, leaning over her, kisses her

on the mouth while playing, with one hand, with the jet of urine running into the bowl. The two girls admit to each other that this is far better than with the stone statue in the red goldfish pool and they are sorry they cannot tarry longer. Next, the scented steam of the shower where Odile attentively washes her princess's lissome body, then she strokes the lash marks on her ass and inner thigh with a healing balm.

102. When they arrive at dinner they are dazzling. The mistress has donned, mined from Odile's vast professional wardrobe, a schoolgirl's outfit, of the underage slut sort favored by gentlemen, with no underwear whatsoever. As for Odile, she has chosen a minuscule, white, sexy maid's apron that covers just half her belly: a pink silk ribbon holds it in place above her belly button, while the outer ruffle allows glimpses of her russet muff at the slightest move, and additionally of the top of her thighs up to the frilly pink garters holding up her white lace stockings, worn without shoes. On her back side, under the large bow, her ass, still adorned by the indispensable bright pink lash marks left by Sorel, is plainly exposed, in the same way that her breasts, the size of tiny apples, also remain naked, ready to be whipped, by Gigi this time.

103. At the table, in her father's company, this latter at first behaves like a reserved young lady, dignified, conscious of her rank. Then, the alcoholic beverages relaxing the atmosphere, a few remarks about her servant's pretty backside, unjustly mistreated, lead her to want to show herself next to Odile, both looked at from the back, so that the professor might compare the affronts they have undergone. Like Gigi, she too, is wearing not a hint of underwear, all she need do is lift her short, loose, pleated, tartan skirt to the top of her groins to display the serious whip-marks in turn stigmatizing her. At the father's request they move closer to him so as to be within reach. The very free nature and perfectly casual tone of these exchanges leave him brimming with optimism for what lies ahead. He delicately fondles the marks on the two young women's

bottoms, but also, in the servant's case, her anal bud and her russet muff. Odile spreads her thighs to facilitate things, should he wish to explore her vulva in greater detail.

104. Able to appreciate, as a connoisseur, the quality of the lashings on both girls, he asks his daughter what made her deserving of such severe punishment; the schoolgirl replies innocently that they were playing at reproducing the large photograph of Violetta about which they had spoken at noon. Back at the table, she asks, as though it were the most ordinary of questions, if her mother used to let herself be sodomized. Sensing a favorable terrain for other developments or exercises, he doesn't have to be asked twice: "When I began to subject her to it, Violetta was certainly not your mom. She must have been twelve, a virgin on both sides, I could only have penetrated her anus by force. It hurt her and she would cry in shame each time, which is not at all disagreeable for a rapist, as you have often read in your schoolbooks. I was very taken with her and wanted to make her happy, but I had, nevertheless, bought her from her parents with the explicit intention of inflicting this on her, and worse still, obviously.

105. "Then, quite quickly, she agreed sweetly to submit to it, but on condition that it be to punish her, and preferably after tying her up in a degrading position. Her mouth, on the other hand, I had been making use of from the start, without any difficulties: sucking my cock entertained her, the ejaculation fulfilled her as compensation of her efforts and she swallowed sperm without displaying the slightest distaste. After her twelfth birthday, her little pubescent muff was turning velvety and golden. On her rear, thanks to lubricant, to my gentleness when required, and to her increased sensuality, she came to take real pleasure in sodomy. The humiliation persisted, but henceforth, it was a part of her clitoroanal pleasure. This love, said to be against nature, suited us both, since above all, she insisted on remaining a virgin until our nuptials. When she turned fifteen, we married. But I did not deflower

her immediately, the sadism for which my young spouse had developed a proclivity, perversely, was alimented by her virginity."

106. After dessert, Gigi removes Odile's little apron and her lace stockings, and she ties her hands behind her back. The father, amused, asks her the reason. His daughter explains that this is the sad fate of maids once their work is done at the table, in the scullery, or wherever else, they must forthwith undress entirely and be at the disposal of their masters, on their knees most often, their useless arms tied behind their back. It makes it more practical should one want to rape them, or subject them to a few abuses, or make them lick one's sex, for instance. "Isn't that so, you little slut?" she asks the maid, pinching her nipple good-naturedly. "Yes, Madam," she replies, lowering her eyes, modestly. Gigi decides, then, to hand her to her father to do with her as he pleases. And, without further ado, she shoves her doll down between the professor's thighs, who distractedly caresses her mouth, then the inside of her vulva, shiny with juices after the fondling to which her charms have been submitted in the course of presenting dinner and wine to her young mistress, kept quite busy by her new servant.

107. Sorel has left his friend yet another personal gift: a box of Romeo y Julieta cigars, of the *robusto* variety. He is getting ready to light one, but deems it insufficiently humidified. Odile, accustomed to gentlemen, in spite of her very recent initiation, does not need it spelled out. So she prepares to shift her balance, spreads her knees and raises one of her legs to press her calf on the smoker's thigh, who assists her with one hand in finding a more stable position. Her little pussy with its red muff is now at the right height, easy access for burying the uncut tip of the Havana cigar. As the adolescent is not a virgin, the entire fragile tobacco cylinder can be made to penetrate her cunny, ideally humid, for a very gentle to and fro, held open with two prudent fingers by the father, meticulous as ever, who then raises it to his nostrils. Satis-

fied with the result, he makes his daughter smell it, too. Then he cuts its rounded tip with his teeth and lights the other end deliberately. "Delicious," he says drawing a few fragrant drags. When the incandescent tip is good and red he moves it close to the servant's breast to graze its areola. The girl, accustomed it would seem, to this homage, barely allows her flinching to show at the fleeting burn, but immediately recovers her disarming slave's smile.

108. Evoking memories of his youth in the army, at a time when the harsh laws of war still recalled ancestral military customs, the father, who is savoring long puffs of the Odilized Julieta, wistfully recounts for his young daughter the fate awaiting girls taken prisoner during the sack of conquered cities. The tender gesture he had just performed with the Havana cigar upon the sweet consenting breast has reminded him that it used to be customary, concerning the arousing fillies selected specially in view of their torture, after the victory feast they had served naked to the officers, to burn their still-intact charms carefully while smoking cigars, only then deflowering them, and then making them perish, as a group, or one after another, by interminable tortures. To satisfy Gigi's legitimate curiosity concerning the warrior's repose after combat, he shares old reminiscences while humidifying the Havana again from time to time, at the risk of inflicting a few fiery scrapes on Odile's proffered quim, still in the same position. "Everyone should admit this is the best way to humidify a cigar!" he declares, "the two scents are so well matched."

109. Very moved, as she always is, by tales of torture, all the more so in this case where her dear papa is the protagonist, the schoolgirl expresses her regret, in chaste terms, at never having witnessed the burning of the breasts of a captive impaled on his cock. And she tries to imagine the marvelous finale of thirty-six girls sacrificed together, hung by their ankles all around the rotunda where the feast was held, side by side, their legs very widely spread, each girl's right foot tied to her neighbor's left, the three dozen genitals

cleaved with four or five saber blows, and the blood flowing in abundance onto bodies contorting in pain for an hour or two at least, before expiring, the circular skewer forming a graceful, red curtain, swaying in the breeze.

110. But our studious novice, ever more stimulated, must presently take the humidor doll back to her prison. No point freeing her hands since this is how she will sleep. Her mistress, therefore, forces her to pee, then to wash, with her arms chained behind her back, which involves all sorts of lascivious contortions and a few lashings, at times presenting insurmountable obstacles that make the prisoner laugh. As for the inside of her sex meanwhile, Gigi, good little princess that she is, takes care of it herself, and with brutal insistence. Next, under the pretext of the excessive heat, due no doubt to the proximity of the *fornax*, she swiftly slips out of her dress, the only thing she is wearing, and lays on the bed on her back. Her knees bent and raised, her thighs apart, her feet resting on the edge of the mattress, she starts nervously manipulating her clitoris.

111. On an imperious signal addressed to her servile attendant, now more or less clean, this latter kneels against the bed, leaning forward to kiss her tyrannical accomplice's blazing sex, Gigi takes this opportunity to ensnare her shoulders between her raised legs, while squeezing the docile head and grabbing its red curls to shove the full mouth for which she has been longing against her vulva, so brusquely that Odile, unable to use her hands, can't at first gain access. "Lick it, you stupid whore!" Gigi snaps impatiently, in the grip of her fantasy, seeing appear before her a double of the servant hanging by her feet. Her father, immense in his black pajamas, stands behind the victim, brandishing his cavalry saber (the one in the attic that used to scare her so when she was little) whose razor-sharp, gleaming blade sinks in slow motion, once, twice, inside Odile's gashed pubis, this same Odile whose tongue and lips have, at present, found their mark, and who is sucking

the clitoris to the best of her abilities. At the seventh saber blow, rivulets of scarlet blood spurt onto her belly and her breasts. And Gigi begins to come, with a hoarse rattle, as though she herself had just been riven at her core.

112. Decimated by this *petite mort* of immeasurable duration, she goes back to the great conjugal bed as though sleepwalking, without washing or putting any clothes back on. As soon as she perceives her father in his black pajamas, laying on his back, reading an old book, she rushes toward this sanctuary and lays on top of him. He says tenderly, "You smell of come," sets down the volume he was holding in both hands, and holds the trembling body whose enamored flesh rubs itself against his chest and belly, more lasciviously than usual. Recovering what is rightfully his with feeling, he fondles her little round ass, which happens to be right under his hand and that has been his since time immemorial. Having encountered the anus he deliberately caresses its sluice. Little by little, the young girl is appeased. She says, finally, in a hesitant, timid voice: "If you were to put your finger in my secret rose would one have to call it sodomy?" "No," replies her playful tutor, "for that something altogether different would have to be put inside!" "And what if you were to put two of your fingers in there?"

113. In fact, he really wouldn't mind trying right away, given how pliable she seems, how ready to take the next step. But he has no lubricant on hand ... And besides, Gigi is visibly dropping from exhaustion. He is about to leave the bed to let her rest when the adolescent, in the drowsiness that is rapidly overcoming her, mumbles languidly that she would like her sweet papa to go and rape the servant in her dungeon, whose door is unlocked. The little whore is naked, her hands bound behind her back and a foot chained to the bed. He should take her in whatever way suits him, regardless of her wishes, but she would like it if at the end, after slapping her until she cries, he spills his sticky come all over

her face, sullying her as much as possible. She won't be able to wash afterwards, since, not knowing the code for unlocking them, he will not have undone her chains. "Why not," he thinks. As he's leaving the room to acquit himself of this mission, Gigi is already fast asleep, worn out by this exceptionally full day, with the legendary innocence of angelic little girls who love their parents, work hard at school, and are able to recite the lessons they have been taught perfectly.

114. At the end of this remarkable day, the father has decided to reestablish the organization of the household according to the model Violetta had instituted. Pleased, no doubt, with the night of love with Odile, he wants to start by acquiring new boarders, on the one hand for the four *deliciae* that remain vacant, on the other hand for the traditional concubines' harem—for favorites or simple slaves—that has long fallen into disuse. He wants, lastly, to restore the two dormitories for little girls, indispensable to servicing a vast old-fashioned home that every evening receives guests who are practitioners of pleasure, not to mention the great feasts celebrating birthdays, communions, marriages, notable deflowerings, etc. Let us remember the most frequent source for these supplies: detention centers for little girls where lost children, abandoned or runaway children, or those who have been kidnapped are sold; servants' fairs for buying ones whose ages range from nine to seventeen, and who have quickly turned into a market for bedfellows, captive girls delivered as war trophies who are anywhere from seven to nineteen years old, and are auctioned off to individuals, adolescent virgin girls, newlyweds, child-women breastfeeding babies, as well as princesses of royal blood and imported young women sentenced to death.

115. The following day's luncheon is served very late, which happens rarely. The daily local paper, in its calendar of sales, auctions, and traveling markets carries an ad announcing an exceptional sales event taking place that very evening, the exceptional sale of an en-

tire religious boarding school specializing in the sexual education of pretty girls of high rank trained for happy marriages. Taken captive in an enemy state where the upper classes speak French, they have no identity papers and can therefore be sold "for all uses." The transactions, access to which is not free, will take place at a historic chateau in the vicinity, in the middle of a dense forest surrounded by high fences. Bedecked in an aura of mystery, its inhabitants are never visible, other than a pack of huge black dogs that bark ferociously. The professor instantly decides to go, and to take along his two schoolgirls, who are delighted by the adventurous nature of this outing.

116. So, the father harnesses the old horse—rather slow but still good looking—to the best maintained of the carriages, testaments to a past glory. In the absence of a coachman, he himself drives, perched on the raised front seat. The two girls, dressed with care, attract the gaze of onlookers. Sitting side by side on the wide, padded leather backseat, they primly hold each other's hands, without making too great a show of their curiosity for these new places. Both sides of the tall ironwork gate have been opened, a rare event. The father pays the high entrance fee only for himself, the young ladies are admitted without having to pay, regardless of whether or not they are for sale. The event (it appears that what will unfold is a sophisticated reception) will take place in the chateau's newest wing, dating from the early nineteenth century, with an impressive view overlooking the ancient, medieval, fortified section that is solid without a single breach and that, in fact, is a prison, a rather unusual one. One immediately notices, in the sumptuous salons, young people earmarked to serve the pleasure of buyers who retain their winsome boarding school uniforms modified to a lighter, more summery version, given the stormy heat hanging over them this end of July.

117. Smiling and graceful, the girls circulate among groups of elegant gentlemen to deferentially offer trays laden with champagne

flutes, small dainty cakes, or canapés. The only strange thing up to this point would be that these men, who among one another, are exceedingly polite, display no restraint, not just in gawping at the pretty waitresses without the least discretion, but also in touching them, at times in quite indecent ways. If one of them should wish it, the designated girl sets down her tray on a small pedestal table so that her admirer can undo a part of her tight-fitting little dress to fondle her breasts, her sex, her ass, her crotch, kiss her lips, ask her to take up various poses, all the more lewd given she is wearing nothing underneath, not the tiniest shred of a lingerie item. The girls accept this wantonness as entirely natural, receiving the most brazen gestures without relinquishing their perfectly sweet demeanor, with a perfect dose of bashful emotion. Small rooms with sofas have even been foreseen so that a selected schoolgirl can undress altogether, with a view to more intimate adulation, without however, compromising her virginity.

118. More striking still, certainly in a bourgeois setting, are the living statues on display here and there. All of them are constructed using the same model, an entirely naked, adolescent girl, facing forward, nailed in an X to a cross, her body pierced in various interesting spots by arrows, and buckling in pain, like female Saint Sebastians embellished by the fresh blood that flows from their wounds. To stifle their moans and maintain a pleasant, appropriately hushed atmosphere, their mouths have been stuffed with large bloody lingerie tampons. Some of the co-disciples of the objects on sale are sacrificed to spread a healthy terror among the captives, which explains the group's, on the whole, excellent conduct. Several of those crucified, moreover, appear to be dying.

119. A handsome young man with a marked English accent approaches Gigi, who is still holding hands with Odile dressed in the sexy schoolgirl outfit her mistress was wearing the previous evening, both are fascinated by a display where a voluptuous statue with a sweet face, still very much living, is attempting in

vain to move her limbs, succeeding only in enlarging the wounds wrought by the iron nails fixing her to the cross, piercing the palms of her hands and her ankles, as well as a fifth bleeding wound resulting from a short saw-toothed metal pivot atop which her pubic area rests. The pretty girl (of fifteen or sixteen summers) has a discreet brown muff utterly mottled with blood, two arrows having penetrated deep inside her crotch. Gigi, turning to the English young man (he cannot be twenty yet) flashes him a smile of tacit connivance. He ventures to ask if her friend is for sale. "Naturally, sir," she answers, "everything here is for sale. It's simply a matter of paying a high enough price." The boy, very intimidated, hesitates. Gigi carries on, "In any event, the absolute rule is that you can fondle her for free." The affecting torture victim on display having succeeded in displacing her ass slightly on the support that torments her as it also keeps her from fainting, starts bleeding increasingly profusely from her torn vulva, resulting in a small puddle on the ground. "Very pretty, don't you think?" remarks Gigi.

120. Then, addressing Odile, who has just turned around as well, she orders assertively: "Undo your top, you little slut, the young gentleman wants to handle your breasts." The servant says, "Yes, Madam," and performs promptly, though looking frightened. The Englishman blushes, as only they know how, while the obedient schoolgirl spreads aside, using both hands, the unfastened panels of her dress, liberating her marvelous brand new breasts on whose areolas pink makeup has even been applied, as well as a brighter red to the little tips. Then, without awaiting the order, which cannot be long coming, Odile lifts the lower part of her skirt to clearly reveal her flat belly and, in the absence of panties, her delicate russet fur. Gigi grabs the well brought up young man's hand who seems hardly to know what to do with himself, and rubs it against the moist pubic cleft, saying: "She has a very suave and extremely arousing scent. Smell your fingers." The servant, playing along, tearfully implores, "Don't sell me, Mistress, I beg you. You know

perfectly well what they do with their purchases. I don't want to die so soon." "Yes, of course I know... But if he pays enough... Besides, he's not necessarily going to put you to death right away. He'd want to see a return on the money he's spent for a few days. If you go about things right, perhaps a week even."

121. Just then, Gigi notices the professor, who is walking toward them looking pleased, no doubt due to his purchases. "What's more here is our father," she says to the boy, in the throes of new anxieties. "We're glad you've come, my dear father, to save us. This young Englishman seems to understand a bit of French, but he won't accept that your daughters aren't for sale." She is still holding the panicked buyer's hand that she brings to her nose to sniff insistently. "Yes, darling papa," she says, "you came just in time: he was about to deflower her with his huge fingers." The father answers, not in the least ruffled: "If he likes Odile's scent, we could sell her to him virgin, but obviously that will be much more expensive... Plus, come to think of it, I'd rather break her hymen myself, as we'd planned, after first torturing her for a while, it won't be long now, anyway, for you either probably, to see you both suffering next to each other, what an enchanting spectacle for a sentimental father... you do understand, young man. Meanwhile, I've managed to find what we needed here: six little girls, two concubines, and for the *deliciae*, four young women condemned to death. In fact all twelve originate from the same place (the destroyed boarding school) and have the same status. And I've already decided how to use them at home. They'll be delivered to the house, as a precautionary measure, by a constabulary car. For the time being, my little doves are shut away in the jail next door where we'll go and take a look at them."

122. This female penitentiary, adjacent to the chateau, merits a more elaborate visit. Only those are admitted to its secret (and terrifying) premises, who have made major purchases. They gain access from the salons where the auction takes place by way of a subter-

ranean gallery that first opens onto an ancient torture museum, long since shut down. Among the accumulation of bizarre, often monumental objects residing here, gathered over centuries, are torture devices of diverse provenance: Egyptian, Ottoman, Babylonian, Byzantine, Roman, Syrian, Chinese, etc. Gigi would like nothing better than to go around with Odile and have her try out some of the barely comprehensible postures, but their considerable dimensions notwithstanding, the rooms are barely lit, often with a single candle. And the policemen leading them are walking at a fair pace.

123. After passing other spaces that, on the contrary, are entirely empty, as though abandoned, they arrive in a bare, white room, furnished with ten or so very dignified but uncomfortable chairs, like bishop's thrones, a sign on the door indicating, "Waiting room. Delivery of merchandise." There are already three people sitting here: a young fashionable couple, the man, dressed soberly and elegantly, accompanied by a pretty, poised, young woman of the same age (about twenty), wearing a silk evening gown of black tulle, suggestively shredded by some avant-garde designer; the third client is a respectable fat lady holding a thick file of photographs that she flips through distractedly. Perhaps she has made her selections solely on the basis of pictures, as Gigi had not noticed her in the cocktail party's numerous salons comprising an endless display of seven- to sixteen-year-old schoolgirls, the eventual selection of those chosen, their humiliating examination, as well as the particular taste tests imposed.

124. There then enter two uniformed police offers unceremoniously pushing three young ladies in front of them who visibly hail from the same educational institution as the rest of the service providers on sale. They are still in their boarding school dresses and lace-up booties, but there is one radically novel detail in their appearance: all three have their hands chained behind their backs and their ankles, bare above their refined booties, are shackled with thick,

crude, forged iron cuffs linked to a heavy, quite short chain that prevents them from running, or even from walking at all quickly. The young husband stands, looking welcoming and inspects them one by one with a contented air, while holding a slender riding crop with a wide, very supple popper in his right hand. The three captives, adolescents who are barely thirteen or fourteen, are terribly pretty, graceful, visibly shapely. Their more or less unbuttoned uniforms flutter pleasingly from one moment to the next, revealing glimpses of a shoulder, a breast, or even a pubic mound unfettered by panties, since here they are presenting themselves in the state of dishevelment in which they were just chosen by their buyers, at the conclusion of a long session of fondling. Only, heavy chains have been added.

125. Two of them are all smiles, and appear entertained by their fantastical ravishing, curious as to what might follow, and visibly well-disposed. It is easy to understand, seeing them, that the three have been bought as boudoir companions, that they know it, and that two at least have wisely made their peace with this, in the absence of a legitimate husband to whom they might have been destined, who might have turned out ugly, old, and brutal. They allow themselves to be handled with highly promising amiability by their new owner who, to make them turn, bend their knees, spread their thighs, bite down on the flap of a skirt their master has lifted to stuff its hem in their mouth to display their nude bellies, each time gives them a light tap of the whip, barely affecting the flesh, still covered in some spots by the open uniforms. One of the girls, who must be the youngest, judging by the pronounced triangle of her mound, smooth as a nectarine but with a dashingly drawn slit, even manifests, in what is a very successful show of fearful submission, and in spite of being a virgin, naturally, as are the rest of her companions, the loving consideration of a well-trained young wife: the whip having struck her ass especially hard, the amiable prisoner manages with both her hands chained, to lift the entire back of her dress so as to directly proffer her deli-

cious rounded bottom of whose powers of attraction she appears already aware.

126. The buyer, impressed, administers three smart strokes that the adroit girl child accompanies with the affecting pouts of a stricken child, decidedly learned in school. She immediately senses that it has worked, as the master turns her around to passionately kiss her on the lips, while caressing her bruised buttocks with a delicate hand. The mistress, who has remained seated, compliments the good pupil on her sweet manners. But she wants her husband to now bring her the one among the three girls who, on the contrary, appears unhappy and afraid. The lady wants to see, open, and feel her pussy. So, the young man puts her within reach of his wife and displays her entire pretty belly as he had done with the previous girl. This girl is quick to obey, but gracelessly bites down on the fabric with her incisors all the same. She has a trim, discreet, brown muff that is already quite thick. When the mistress brings her hand to it, to rather savagely introduce two fingers inside her vulva, the distressed girl breaks down in tears and opens her mouth to apologize, allowing the fabric to drop.

127. Deciding the ill-mannered apprentice whore must be punished post-haste, the despotic lady orders her to kneel beside her and lift the back of her skirt with her chained hands as her younger cohort had done, and so perfectly. At the same time, half prostrate, she will kiss the mistress's crotch, the top of her bare thigh, through a propitious tear in the black dress. No doubt, she does not do this with sufficient sensuality, for the young man lashes her bottom with all his might while his wife holds the victim still, grabbing her by her vulva, flaying it, unconcerned, with her long nails filed to a point. The girl howls in pain. A guard immediately appears and suggests the buyer, together with her prey, should move to a room for tryouts, or torture even, as the waiting room is intended only for presentations, albeit not exceedingly chaste ones, but

avoiding any perturbing antics. The husband acquiesces without argument.

128. But he then tells the three captives that the young lady to whom they now belong only wants their goods on condition that they succeed in pleasing her in her erotic games. If, on the other hand, they idiotically weep at the slightest privation, their fate will be an altogether different one. They have been bought "for all uses," let us not forget, and their mistress has the right to put them to death whenever she should choose to, and by the most horrendous torments, which risks being sooner in the case of this pretty person who has just behaved in a deliberately stupid manner. They are love objects and as it so happens, amorous pleasures necessarily take cruel forms. This is when three black-clad gentlemen enter, Englishmen all three, one of them walks toward Gigi to ask if he might sit next to her. And before long he engages her in a conversation.

129. "I was watching my son from afar," he says, "and you made a fool of him and with good reason." Then, addressing the older man whom he has only just noticed, and whom he supposes to be her father: "Your girls made my son believe you had come to put them up for sale, and he carried on like an imbecile. We have just come from England, he and I, planning to buy one or two French dolls. He's at that age. He is engaged to a fourteen-year-old virgin and seems to be as much of a nitwit as she is. I believe it's very important for their future together that she grow used to being whipped for no reason, before their wedding even. It used to be quite a widespread practice where we are from, in all good, high society families. And marriages were the stronger for it, people didn't divorce at the drop of a hat. So, for his eighteenth birthday, I'm giving him two virgins, thirteen and fifteen years old, just out of an institution for training young wives, known as far afield as England."

130. At this point, three policemen in uniform appear, accompanying a flock of little girls who seem to be around seven to twelve years old and from a source different than the chic boarding school plundered by our troops. They are all wearing leg irons, identical to the ones worn by the girls delivered to the young couple. But they are all naked, and a supplementary chain joins them to one another in a lovely swerving skewer that the guards point in the direction of the fat lady. She promptly begins to count them, one by one, against a register, checking who knows what in her photographic file. There are eighteen of them appearing before the buyer in descending order of age, to recite, in quite marked Central European accents, simple sentences they must have learned in prison. They look to have lovely figures and their young bodies, judiciously nourished but without excess, awaken the carnal appetites. At first glance, they come across as having been less deliberately hewn for pleasure than the schoolgirl servers sold in the salons.

131. The first girl steps forward and, trembling, says, "My name is Fabiola, I'm thirteen years old, I am a virgin. I have not yet had my period." She has pretty blond down covering her pubis and minuscule nascent breasts. "That is not all," the lady says softly, awaiting a shameful detail, hard to utter. The child speaks again, a little more quietly: "My father has been sodomizing me for the last six months, once a week only, when I come home from the religious school to spend Sundays at home. He accuses me of putting poison in his coffee. It's not true, of course, but I've nevertheless been sentenced to death." She bursts into desperate sobs, then, in spite of her tears, adds, with effort, "I know speaking French quite well." She is so affecting and at the same time attractive with her sweet, downy, helpless muff that Gigi regrets not having been able to buy her at what was likely a very low price.

132. The English gentleman explains to her father that the fat lady is a friend of his, involved in retail resale in Germany and France

(she is German). The little girls she will take with her have been sentenced to death, are more or less guilty, imported from Moravia. They will not necessarily be executed. All of them, without exception, will be subjected to various customary rapes, not always accompanied by torture. Afterwards, the least gifted will work as anonymous slaves in sewing factories. The prettiest will be placed in houses of pleasure, and sometimes, admittedly, of very cruel pleasures. Criminal or not, the delivery of the girls, in chains and entirely naked, is the norm here, no matter their origin, and is generally believed to play a part in the client's arousal. This must not be true in the case of the austere German lady who pays the little girls no erotic attention whatsoever, not even to the most appetizing, whom she could partake of in whatever way might have suited her.

133. As for Gigi, beguiled by the spectacle, she, in any case, shares the general opinion that their defenseless nakedness, along with their restrictive chains, imparts the impression they are being led to torture, which necessarily adds to their sexual allure. Surprising herself by her own (recently acquired) audacity, she shares this appreciation with the Englishman sitting next to her, who is of the same opinion and who offers, if horrible torture sessions performed on pretty girls are of interest to the professor and the distinguished young ladies, to take them to specialized venues and to let the father know in advance when spectacular performances of real sacrifices are planned at one or another private theater, square with the police, or even once in a while, for one of the dinners called "extremely libertine," so fashionable these days, where the delectable serving girls, ten to sixteen, have been sold by their parents as apprentice whores "for all uses."

134. The girls believe all they will be doing is serving food while naked to rich gentlemen, allowing themselves to be fondled along the way without making a fuss, to be kissed more or less anywhere on their body, or at times agreeing to perform very light sexual ser-

vices, such as receiving gentle lashings, or minute cigar burns on their seductive charms, all par for the course in conjugal love. But the parents know perfectly well that they will not see them again, that they will be drugged to progressively obliterate their instincts of self-preservation, to accept ever more lurid compliments. All, without exception, even the virgins that are far from being nubile, will be raped during the meal, then, frolics and profligacy having overtly swung into horror, they will submit to forcible tortures, soon intolerable, and will be put to death one by one. This is how families that are too numerous find an opportunity to definitively place surplus little girls, and alas, especially the prettiest ones for whom higher official prices have been designated, rather than spending on a costly dowry to deliver them to problematic husbands without warranties.

135. As for the girls whom the father is acquiring today, he can use and abuse them as much as he wants, make them perish by torments of his choosing, or even resell them, (no surcharge will be imposed). He can lend them to friends who will have whatever powers he accords them: to fondle, make love, torture them, etc. But if he prostitutes them, that is to say, if he receives money or gifts in exchange for these pleasures, even if it is just to watch them be tortured, he must declare his home a commercial business in advance, and acquit himself of all the applicable taxes and charges for this sort of merchandise. By the same token, in the case of definitive resale, that is exempt from the imposition of plus value taxes, he must nonetheless acquit himself of the taxes on commercial transactions and also declare any sums received in his estate.

136. Let us recap some important points here, relative to the legal status of pleasure girls. Prostitution is permissible according to our law, but procuring is forbidden, other than in two precise cases specified in different, more or less recent rulings. In families, on the one hand, a man is considered the natural owner of his

wife and their female children whatever their age. He, therefore, has the right to prostitute them as he sees fit and without needing their consent. If one of them succeeds in running away, he can have all the forces of the police search and return the girl to her father or husband's home by force, thereafter he is authorized to subject her to whatever appropriate physical punishments, including confinement to a torture dungeon, or execution without trial. Renting out one's spouse or daughters by the day, especially if they are young and attractive, for all erotic uses, in private or on stage, including for real torture displays with actual visible injuries inflicted on a delectable non-consenting subject, which without any doubt provides the best hourly returns, can represent the only stable income for a well-organized head of household. What's more, the sums transferred by clients need not be declared to the fiscal administration, as they are exempt from all tax burdens (revenue, commercial or non-commercial profits, etc.).

137. By the same token, if a young new spouse, or a daughter from a previous marriage, is sold irreversibly, particularly for "all uses, even criminal," the sum acquired in the transaction does not fall into the same category as taxes on wealth, no more than do sums of the capital represented by the presence in the home of a pretty girl not for sale. It seems, moreover, normal that this transfer for a fee should be treated by the owner in the same way as that of one of his own kidneys, in the case of an organ transplant. But this disposition does not apply to adopted children, because it would lead too easily to fraud. Finally, where male children are concerned, the father's proprietary right automatically expires at the boy's majority, that is at age eighteen.

138. The second instance where the interdiction in the trafficking of girls for prostitution is lifted, more dubitably this time, concerns legally declared merchandise businesses. The fat German lady, for example, is nothing but a procurer. But this activity is seen as fully comparable to an enterprise trading in fruit, clothing, jewelry, au-

tomobiles, or any other product commonly used by consumers. The only difference being that the taxes paid (sales tax, business taxes, etc.) are much higher in this case than for other commodities. These resellers who supply professionally registered brothels or crib houses, which scrupulously pay their taxes, social security dues etc., must manage their cash flow prudently, given the pressures by fiscal authorities, they are not in a position to miscalculate their general expenses or they will quickly go bankrupt.

139. Those under scrupulous surveillance by the morality police are the amateur pimps that make girls work outside the legal framework. The best way of finding them in order to inflict heavy fines on them, or a few days in prison even, is to make the young, inexperienced whores who are most often ignorant of the rudimentary laws of their profession, and who believe prostitution to be entirely licit, talk. In fact, it is extremely rare for a girl not to have a protector. So, police officers undertake massive sweeps on hot streets that are the hangouts of titillating girls who need only be interrogated for a couple of days before admitting to giving the lion's share of their take to dandy pimps with whom they are often in love. They are then convicted, not of having sold their bodies, but of supporting a pimp, subjected, for this, to corporal punishments whose sadistic cruelty is so prolonged that they rarely survive them.

140. It is a known fact that the police officers working in special prisons for preliminary interrogations, for the sentencing, and for the execution of punishments, have obtained from their union organizations official recognition of their right to unlimited rapes before, during and after the interrogation of all young female suspects under their purview. They are now demanding that the adaptation of prescribed tortures to the personal proclivities of each henchman be considered an additional benefit, and that the same should apply to the duration of the torture. While such legal considerations are being discussed by the father and the English-

man, who appears to be a specialist on these matters (might he be an attorney?), the libertine couple has settled its invoice for the three girls who were delivered. The husband has undone the two youngest girls' shackles freeing them to walk, wrapping the ends of the useless chain around their backsides. Only the restive schoolgirl, who was slow to grasp her current position as fodder for vice, has to hobble heavily, and bloody her feet with every step she takes, however shortened, while also receiving lashings for not moving quickly enough. All three will, however, maintain their ankle irons and continue to have their wrists chained behind their back.

141. Finally, the father's purchases arrive, dressed in their boarding school uniforms, which happened to be included in the agreed price, much higher than what is current, due no doubt to the humiliating, indecent, sexual dressage, as precious to a perverse lover as to a normal spouse. They too wear, on their wrists and ankles, heavy iron chains that identify all the girls sold by the prison, no matter where they had been previously. This is when Odile and Gigi first meet them. The father has carefully buttoned their dresses back up after his fastidious examination of their anatomy. But their arms tied behind their backs, and the excessively short chains at their feet, accentuate their fearful air of good little captives, dreading what lies ahead. They are, at least, pleased to note that the old gentleman who chose them is accompanied by two pretty girls, one of whom, who has remained seated, appears to be the real mistress, whereas the other has risen to greet them, wearing a boarding school uniform comparable to theirs, though different. She kisses each one on the lips, or on a cheek, depending on which they offer.

142. Gigi, who, as stated, has remained seated, finds them so appetizing, desirable, and eliciting of both caresses and the whip, that she claps at their arrival. She nonetheless regrets, she murmurs to her beloved papa, rigid on the chair next to hers, that they are not

delivered completely naked in their chains. "It's better this way," says the professor, who again gauges his pupil's overnight transformation. "This way you'll have the pleasure, as soon as we're back, of making them undress one at a time, in front of you. I've even, for this purpose, put all their chaste schoolgirl underwear back on, after subjecting their intimate graces, which you plan to unreservedly enjoy, to various trials. You won't be disappointed, I promise." There are, in the lot, six little girls for service, aged seven to twelve, two sultanes who will soon turn fifteen ("just like you," he remarks), and four girls sentenced to death, who will occupy the dungeons of delights. The children in this latter group are respectively twelve, thirteen, thirteen and a half, and fourteen summers. "You may, you and Odile may, torture them as you see fit, without needing to ask my permission. To this end, I'm keeping the sultanes for myself." Gigi notes that her father has changed too, as though relieved of a burden, and happy.

143. The gracious Englishman, who had disappeared, returns accompanied by a plain-clothes policeman who will drive the professor and his two girls promptly (as required by the penitentiary administration) to an interrogation chamber where, at that very moment, several young prostitutes, convicted of supporting pimps, are being interrogated and will no doubt be cruelly punished. Gigi accepts delightedly and her father asks that his own captives be delivered to their home that evening. At the farthest point of the oldest of the underground chambers, dating from the Roman era, according to the functionary, the visitors arrive at a vaulted room with massive pillars, vast and seemingly delimited only by the densest shadows, which are further accentuated by thick curls of vapor drifting up from the ground. According to the guard, this place, nicknamed "Hell," is situated on an almost extinct volcanic fault, the deleterious effervescence of whose still-smoldering streams is reputed to make criminals confess against their will. The heat here, in any case, is intense, heavy, and the roiling turbulence evokes the devil's cauldron, more so as the moaning of the

damned is replaced by the desperate cries of adolescent girls and young women being tortured, whose hallucinatory wails resound under the vaulted ceilings.

144. Here and there scenes stand out from the shadows, brightly lit by directional floodlights. The first that the group approaches depicts the final phase of Zizette's torture, the cicerone explains. She is fourteen and a half. Deflowered by her sweet papa, in whose arms she slept since the age of two, almost; in love with him and progressively awakened to pleasure, she had become ever more enticing. Alas, her impecunious father sold her to a two-bit pimp who rented her by the night through a clandestine catalog, as a sort of luxury call girl, just barely pubescent. She thinks she is safe, because of her intimate relations with rich businessmen and well-known ex-ministers. But the police, having discovered that it was not her father prostituting her, arrested her and she has been tortured for the last three days, not counting a part of the nights. She is such a hit that everyone wants a piece of her and the policemen are making this preliminary phase of her punishment last as long as possible.

145. She confessed to everything far too quickly, whereas her inquisitors especially enjoy lying on a bed and having their sex licked by the child prostitute while her anus, vulva, and the surrounding area are burned with cigarettes by underlings. Between sessions, they rape her in both natural orifices; at that time they might singe her breasts, armpits, and belly with a cigar. Her tears flow abundantly, but charmingly, and in the continued hope of an intervention by a well-placed friend, she obeys, weeping, the cruelest of commands so perfectly that all her dainty charms are beginning to show serious damage. Condemned, ultimately, to being burned alive (by a slow fire) for incest, passive pedophilia, procuring and the corruption of politicians, she now finds herself in a position close to that of interrogations: kneeling, her thighs spread wide, her chest half-raised, her hands pulled obliquely to-

ward the vaulted ceiling by steel hooks, a small charcoal brazier placed at her inner thigh, at the right height to gradually consume her fine brown fur, her pubic mound, her perineum, the lowest point of her buttocks, the silky crook of her thighs. Gigi is very moved, she kisses her on the lips passionately, as they finish ravaging her breasts with red hot pokers.

146. While leading them to the next scene, the functionary on call informs his guests that the death penalty having been abolished, it will be necessary, in less than an hour, once the tortured woman's plaintive cries become so feeble as to no longer be heard, to remove the brazier from between her thighs so she might perish naturally, which might take a while longer. But he adds that the policemen, talented amateur photographers, have, since the arrival of the splendid looking Zizette, taken numerous photographs of the child woman being tortured, which will appear in all the luxury magazines devoted to sadistic pedophile pleasures. A large-format book might even be published where the magnificent images will be accompanied by a foreword written by a renowned author.

147. Naked, like all the others, the next actress is Maroussia, an adorable milky redhead who has lived eighteen summers, with a saintly face and fleshy charms, breastfeeding her thirteen-month-old baby girl. She recovered from the birth so quickly that she has regained her almost perfect figure, barely noticeably rounder in the breasts, in particular. An altogether classic case in modern society, she prostitutes herself for the subsistence of a lazy husband whom she loves, and additionally now for their baby. Her only mistake was not marrying this boy officially. "What's the point?" she used to say. And there was no shortage of clients to take the young mother from behind while her little girl, crawling on the floor, tried to grab a nourishing tit, and succeeded when the mother was limber enough. She too, in any case, has her acolytes. She has been raped and her breasts have been lashed this last week, often on her knees, her hands tied behind her back until pearls of

blood appear on her extremely fragile, creamy skin and blend with the milk seeping from the pores of her hardened breasts. Maroussia lets them do as they will with her, bravely, since she has been promised in return that she will finally be allowed to breastfeed her starving baby, a long time coming for both mother and child.

148. Day by day, however, the baby's cries grow more frenzied, for there is too much blood mixed in the milk. Since the accused young woman has not yet admitted to the initial charge (that her companion, to whom she gives all her earnings, is not really her husband), her torturers, wearying a bit of her, of her lacerated breasts and her shrill progenitor, decide to scare her and announce that they are going to have them both quartered, starting with the innocent little girl. The mother is promptly placed in a suitable position, her almost intact body, breasts aside, seen from above, and head on, is lifted thirty centimeters above the ground by an erect metallic phallus, whose terrifying gland has been stuffed inside her anus. To allow greater berth for the contortions and spasms that are bound to ensue, her arms are simply tied behind her back. And her burnished gold hair falls on the crude tiles around her terrorized face. Her legs are spread unimaginably wide, almost in the splits, by means of two winches that pull her feet in opposite directions. Not needing a machine to inflict the same punishment on her, three men have seized the infant, two of them lift her, each holding a foot, to stretch her thighs apart horizontally in a line. To stifle her cries, a punishment pear is put in her mouth. Maroussia, crazed with pain and in despair, wants to confess to her crime. To muzzle her by force, she too is gagged with an enormous oakum tampon, imbibed in the blood of her daughter, whom the third policeman has just deflowered with a knife, while the first two continue to disarticulate her legs.

149. Efficient and discreet photographers snap away countless more pictures, all without a flash, of course. So the condemned can better see the quartering of little Marie, the fruit of sin, the two

men still holding her by her ankles, upside down, now stand over her mother's belly, while a third delivers a few dry lashes with a butcher's cleaver to the little girl's groin in order to properly carve her pubis. Blood now floods Maroussia's yawning sex, and yet more blood after one of Marie's legs is yanked off altogether. Two huge black police dogs, held firmly on a leash by their masters, have appeared, and not by chance, needless to say. The palpitating remains of the accursed child are thrown to them. These beasts must be fed regularly with girls who are still alive, so they conserve the memory of the delicious scent and flavor of the thing that it is their mission to hunt down. The two dogs, next, must clean up, to the last drop, the blood tainting Maroussia's lower belly and all around it, that is, her belly button, her golden muff, the inside of her vulva. As soon as all this is perfectly clean, her own progressive quartering can be resumed. The joints start creaking. Under Gigi's awe-struck gaze, the beautiful victim contorts in voluptuous suffering.

150. Once her thighs are partially torn off, as the guilty whore is beginning to faint, the dogs are given permission to devour her, partially at least (given the obligation to prolong her suffering until she perishes by herself). The beasts begin by tearing off large chunks of the milky flesh of her breasts. Next comes her russet mound (for which they are always avid), the dimple of her groins, her inner thighs. Gigi herself is as hungry as a wolf. She suddenly remembers the legendary text that had made such a sensual impression on her in her pedagogical readings at age twelve. A rich gentleman from Cotentin raised redheads, in the principal aim (though, certainly, not exclusively) of savoring them more or less rare, noting in his journal that they, like does hunted by hounds, are all the more flavorful for having been tortured at great length before being put to death, whereas, on the contrary, up until that time, a life of comfort and affection must be arranged for them, be it in vast cages, or better yet, in gardens surrounded by high, barely visible, iron gates: they must be kissed lasciviously, covered

in intimate caresses, made love to in very gentle ways, they are to be danced with (always naked) to languorous music, taught all the games of Lesbos. When one was selected to be eaten, or for whatever other purpose, it was essential, at all costs, to avoid the slightest anxiety or suspicion among her companions. Their horrible sacrifice would be all the more arousing for it.

151. But the cicerone now insists on showing the two visibly enthusiastic adolescent girls and their papa, just a bit further along, a precious mother of twenty, Blanche, being tortured at the same time as her daughter, Blandine, who has just celebrated her ninth birthday, side by side on identical trestles. They are both ravishing natural blonds, all the more touching as they resemble each other like twins, in spite of the evidently rather different maturity of their charms. Blanche lives with a libertine who is not Blandine's father, and she suspects him of being a little too interested in the little girl, who, moreover, is a tease who is already a graceful sex object for all who delight in nymphs not yet fully bloomed. If the mother has been prostituting her child for the last several months to all their friends and acquaintances, it is in the double aim of depreciating the little girl's body, offered to all comers (and consentingly, to boot), and also to furnish her profligate lover with an income. Blanche does not, as per our laws, have any proprietary rights to Blandine, and neither does the fake father. So the young woman and her daughter are jointly charged with running a clandestine prostitution operation.

152. Hence, both have been placed on all fours atop the sharpened, cutting edge of a pair of thick, steel blades, horizontal and parallel, set a meter or slightly further apart, the child's left ankle has been closely chained to the mother's right ankle. Each woman's other leg, pulled out laterally, not to the extreme, to obtain a symmetrical opening of their thighs, possible as they are of similar heights: Blanche has the adult format of a statue, whereas her daughter, who is growing quickly, will soon be taller than her. Their hands

are already raised to the same level, pulled rather loosely toward the vaults by iron fingers that rigidly enclose their thumbs, so they are not tempted to hang, for relief from their bodily weight, onto the vicious crest of the trestles. The soles of their feet are being burned by light touches from a red-hot poker. And grazing on any part of the plantar hollow is all that is needed for the two relatively free limbs, joined at the ankles, to tremble in concert, and for the two vulvas to be carved further each time, spilling yet more fresh blood.

153. If someone wishes to rape them, they are removed from their torture trestles and placed next to one another on a large bed with white sheets, already patterned scarlet by the placement of their shredded sexes. They weep and moan, but without any aggressiveness following the injections to their vocal chords, since they already confessed a few days earlier, the little girl having first admitted that the man that ends up with the money is not her father at all, which the police had known all along. When Gigi sees them, the next phase of their torture is about to begin, replacing the red-hot poker under the soles of their feet with long metal needles, transpiercing the relevant fleshy parts and the hypersensitive articulations of the two delicate bodies, which one might imagine still intact, were it not for two growing puddles of blood that a hemolytic agent prevents from coagulating, forming on the tiles right beneath the two tortured sexes. One can see, moreover, from time to time the scarlet liquid streaming down the vertical face of the steel blades, then drip, drop by drop, which Gigi appreciatively points out to her confidante.

154. A young police officer, a sunny, handsome fellow, has noticed the two pretty visitors' sustained interest in these unfolding proceedings. He graciously offers that Gigi should place the first needle in Blanche's superb breasts, set high and proud, which the adolescent executes with delectation, on the right areola, skewering it from side to side. Ardent pearls of blood emanate from

the tiny wounds. After the second piercing by the novice, which slowly traverses the two milky globes one after the other, making the chained, tortured girl contort and cry out, the gallant police officer moves closer to his accomplice and in a low voice makes a second proposition: he can, should she wish it, fondle her sex under her dress, or sodomize her even, while she carries out the torture, an arrangement that is often much enjoyed here by ladies of all ages, allied to influential dignitaries from various police forces. The girl is utterly mortified by the ease with which the young man proffers this obscenity, as though it were an ordinary and anodyne entertainment. But she allows no aspect of her profound dismay to show and evenly answers, in a tone at once worldly and friendly, "No thank you, not this evening, it's impossible: I'm with my sister and my husband." And without even taking the precaution of doing so discreetly, she points to her father, who, in spite of his rigid professorial bearing, has introduced his left hand inside Odile's open blouse to touch his own personal mannequin on the same exact spots where the bleeding holes were left by the needles.

155. Without betraying the slightest bitterness, the affable tormentor makes Gigi a third proposal, adding that the delicious little girl, herself condemned to death by torture, has been spared the red-hot irons: the interrogators, who tremendously enjoyed raping her in a reasonable quantity of blood, fearing she might overly damage her anus and cunt by too impetuous a dance on the iron blades. The debutante torturer remembered, regarding the young mother, her real culpability (was she not responsible for the child's torment?), which liberated her, she thought, of all moral scruples. But now she must show that her hand no longer trembles when dealing with the pretty, frivolous little girl, whose innocence merely presented a supplemental attraction to a hardened torturer. So she buries her needle deep into several very painful spots, pulling it out again each time: into the groins, the pubis, the armpits, the waist, the hips... The little girl is wracked with convulsions

of a suffering so acute that her vulva streams blood. Gigi calms her incoherent spasms with a couple of slaps so well-directed that the child gasps and thereafter appears thoroughly extinguished. To revive her, they must resume the perforations across her body, to the accompaniment of the same voluptuous moaning, and a renewed spurting of bright blood now flowing along her inner thighs. A delicate bright red trickle also dribbles out of her half-open mouth, blending with her tears and falling on to her chest as her eyes sink away.

156. Gigi, ecstatic, watches steadily. But a guard appears to say that visitors must now leave these premises, in theory forbidden, and moreover, that they must leave Blandine to die a natural death, while Blanche's torture will carry on as long as necessary. The professor congratulates his decidedly transformed pupil. He has heard her exchange with the enterprising young policeman. These special prisons for sexual delinquents are really a dream come true! The good pupil respectfully asks for permission to kiss the nice, obliging police officer before leaving. Her father deems that this would indeed be proper. The attractive boy returns Gigi's kiss with such ardor that she is utterly dazed: it is even better than in books. We must not forget that her entire life long, this is the only young man she has ever kissed on the lips, so once again, a grand premiere!

157. Odile has gone ahead of her masters to call for the car to come to the medieval building, which takes a while. When she finally returns, her mistress scolds her harshly for slowness, justified nonetheless by the congestion of cars and coaches. The servant apologizes and, looking contrite, opens the right-hand side door to the coach. Then she helps her climb the step stool, while assisting with her cumbersome long dress, meanwhile the father settles in the front seat. When she, in turn, climbs in, it is to sit modestly on the floor, on her knees, at the feet of her capricious mistress. "Stroke me!" orders this latter, whose skirt, which falls

all the way to the floor, is so ample that Odile can easily slip her head and shoulders inside it. But she deems it more desirable, at the moment, to abstain from such familiarity. Gigi, as might have been expected, is not wearing any underwear, and her sweet little pussy is as wet as can be, moved as she is by the all too brief stroll through the torture caverns where justice is exacted. Abruptly, the young woman sits up and pointing to a pile of blankets stacked against the other door (the one on the left-hand side) she says, "There is someone in there watching us."

158. While the carriage was getting on its way, maneuvering with some difficulty, a narrow gap in the pile of plaids and other travel blankets had, seemingly, widened. Between two folds of fabric, deliberately separated, there appeared eyes shining with an anguish that to Gigi signaled the presence of a clandestine passenger. The mistress, in a brisk move, unmasks the new passenger who turns out to be female, a frail little girl of twelve, entirely naked apart from her leg irons and the chains identifying her as a penitentiary prisoner (for dressage and interrogation), no doubt on the run. At the clipped order: "Stand, whore!" the child, curled up in a ball, straightens her body with surprising grace, in order to stand tall, slender but shapely, visibly prepubescent in spite of the sensuality of her pretty, little girl-like manner, vulnerable, terrorized, imploring. Her arms are tightly chained behind her back, as per the rules, but the chain between her feet is slack enough for her to walk almost normally. "Are they searching for you?" asks Gigi, somewhat mollified by the fugitive's troubling charm. "Yes, Madam, they want to put me to death by horrible torture." "Are you a virgin?" "Yes, Madam ... They pretended to sodomize me with a knife, but they were saving me for more dreadful things." Odile interjects, herself trembling at her own guilty temerity, "She's not even eleven. They can't have anything against her. It's simply for their own pleasure that they were preparing to skin her alive, just like they did that other little girl before our very eyes. Don't make her get out, Mistress. I beg you!"

159. The Victoria has stopped at a roadblock where tense guards are searching several vehicles that were already waiting there, before letting them drive on to the gate. Without hesitating, Gigi signals to the little girl to hide under her full skirt, which task she executes with remarkable agility. She is so slight that one would certainly not suspect there might be a fugitive between the young lady's knees, beneath the light fabric whose folds Odile arranges for still greater peace of mind. A minute later, two men open the left-hand door and rummage through the pile of blankets. One says, by way of apology, "A prisoner sentenced to death has escaped. We must prevent her from leaving the grounds." "Seen nothing around here," Gigi replies tranquilly. As soon as the coach is moving at a good trot in the open countryside, she spreads her thighs just wide enough for the prisoner's face to be buried in her intimacy. Then, without any trouble, she guides her unforeseen travel companion to the right spot, where her ferreting mouth promptly sets about softly licking the drenched vulva like a grateful little cat.

160. The twelve servants "for all uses," acquired by the father on the auction block are delivered in a police paddy wagon. They arrive at their destination shortly after the masters themselves. The captives have been left in their schoolgirl uniforms, along with the irons and chains worn at the special prison. The little clandestine licker, fraudulently ravished, is incorporated into this lot, subject to the same heavy ties of servitude, albeit naked. The professor and his daughter sit in the most prestigious armchairs of the formal living room, as though at a tribunal. Odile will serve them drinks while the girls appear before them one after the other, remove all their clothes and lingerie, then kneel, thighs spread wide to succinctly present themselves. Odile has undone their chains to free their feet and hands, which allows them to execute all the orders received: "Arms up ... lift your face ... spread your legs wider ... push your sex forward ... show us the inside of your pussy by spreading the lips properly with your ten fingers ..." Odile,

who is watching a frightened pupil about to break into tears, gives her a little lashing if she doesn't obey quickly enough. If one of her preys delights her exceedingly, Gigi prolongs her examination with injunctions that are more and more revolting until she really starts crying: "Fondle your own clitoris, use a bit of spit if it seems too dry... lie on your back and bend your knees up against your chest while holding your ankles with your legs spread wide so we can see your flower of Sodom under your fluffy muff..." But to punish her for these unnecessary tears, Odile whips her vulva, presented in this manner, yawning, obscene. Then, the innocent victim must apologize.

161. Gigi, meanwhile, has embarked on a series of auditions of her recent protégée, who is already entirely naked, her chains aside. Svelte and slight, aware of arousing the wickedest longings, the seductive gamine, condemned to undergo the cruelest of punishments, walks toward her new mistress, dragging her heavy, useless ankle chains, which serve no purpose other than to stir sensitive souls. She executes a well-practiced curtsy and kneels gracefully, quite happy at the turn events have taken. She talks in sentences that are simple, but admirably correct grammatically, withal denoting intelligence and vivacity. "My first name is Sixty, as I am the sixth of my sisters. Our parents sold me to the "fiancée school" where there was more bedroom science than kitchen science... A sort of sex slave factory. Sometimes it was quite fun. But I had to interrupt my real studies. Now, they call me Sexty, or even Sexie, which points to the future that awaits me."

162. The examiner contemplates her dexterous neophyte with good will, tenderness, and much more even. She says, "Are you sorry?" "I don't know, Madam. I don't know yet... In any case, I'm happy to have been admitted among your erotic playthings." "Are you a virgin?" "Yes, Madam... Only just!" The reply ends on a ravishing grin of good humor. Gigi tells her softly, "Fondle yourself." Prompt and attentive, the child applies herself to the best of her

abilities, moistening her fingers with saliva several times. Then, with a pretty pout of pique, confesses, "It's not working, really, but I'm making progress." "Well then, I'll show you... Private lessons with practical exercises and appropriate punishments." "Yes, Madam. Sorry, Madam. And I love you..." Her last sentence is just barely murmured. Gigi, cutting short any emotion, carries on in an authoritative voice: "Here you will have the rank of sultane. It's more prestigious than 'sentenced to death.' What this privilege means, among other things, is that you shall have to sleep in my father's arms whenever he should want you. It won't be long, obviously, before he picks one of your flowers. And soon, no doubt, the other one as well." "Yes, Madam, it's the very least of things." "Come here you little whore!" (in a very tender voice, once again).

163. Moving forward on her knees, Sexie gets as far as the armchair, where her mistress spreads her legs to receive her. Odile, at a silent signal, binds her arms in chains behind her back again, then, with the leg iron hanging at one of her ankles, she attaches her to a bronze ring, meant for this purpose, on the side of the armchair. Gigi then kisses the little girl on her delectable mouth, amorously, while Odile lashes her bottom with three strokes of the whip, brisk and precise, that, her complete submission notwithstanding, make her tremble, without however interrupting the kiss that is prolonged and is passionately reciprocated by the child. "That is not a punishment, you know, but simply a sign that you are mine. All our captives must be whipped regularly so they don't forget who they belong to." Sexie then remains kneeling between her mistress's knees throughout the parading of schoolgirls. The ardent princess whispers in her beloved's ear, "You kiss as well as you lick, my sweet little slut..." "You see, Madam, that my prostitution institution did have some merit: I learned not only how to satisfy gentlemen, but also their young companions." Gigi, considerately, has a cushion brought for her so she can enjoy the spectacle without leaving her, seated on the floor between her thighs, chained to the imperial armchair. She is even offered a shawl to throw

over her shoulders, unnecessary, as the day's heavy heat has hardly abated.

164. Once all twelve juvenile schoolgirls, now only wearing their slaves' chains and having become simple pleasure objects, have one by one displayed their undeniable charms, been examined in humiliating fashion, compared in various postures, and whipped quite severely, most of them are in tears. They have been forbidden to speak to each other, even by signs, and they exchange anxious or forlorn glances, until, that is, Odile blindfolds them, which adds to their sense of vulnerability and abandonment. But the wide, silk, black band suits them so well, which is precisely why Gigi gets up to kiss the most alluring, to deeply fondle their cunts, mistreat the breasts of the best endowed, and forage in other prospective mounds. Finally, all of them must kneel and the mistress slaps those whose backs are not arched enough or who haven't sufficiently spread their legs. The professor considers that throughout this beginning to the proceedings, the two sultanes have been far too spared by Odile, and by her mistress, respectful no doubt of the father's privilege. His daughter would be grateful to him, indeed, not to waste any time in rectifying this inequity.

165. It is the beautiful Suzanne whom he chooses, blond and rosy, her blue eyes hidden by the black scarf tied over her golden locks. Odile makes her come forward on her knees, all the way to the distinguished master, who promptly draws her against him, making her kiss him on the lips. Already at fifteen, she is an imposing role model, the most accomplished in the harem of nymphets, where she is the oldest. Based on her use of her tongue and her lips, she seems to have acquired excellent training as a sex doll at the boarding school. He asks whether she was often whipped, and for what transgressions. She answers in her sweet still-childish voice with its fruity lilt. The sisters had, she says, a very shocking practice of whipping the girls each time they would get their period, starting on the first or second day, when the bleeding is

the heaviest. Suzanne, at that time, had to remove her little red-stained panties (tampons were strictly forbidden) and give them to the inspecting sister as admission of her guilt. Then she would kneel, unbutton the entire front of her skirt, and lift it with both hands to show her backside, naked from the waist and hips to the garters holding up her thigh-high black stockings, in front of the whole class full of the other schoolgirls who, jealous of her figure and her fair good looks, snickered and made fun of her.

166. "They would stuff my bloody panties of shame in my mouth to stifle my cries, and whip me with a hard crop that hurt terribly. I would be crying in pain and dying of shame as the obscene flux ran between my thighs. If it were not satisfyingly abundant, a few lashes on my lower belly would unleash a fresh flood of it. It was necessary, our confessor said, to drive out the evil inhabiting our bodies by punishing us for being girls. We had committed the original sin and were cursed for all eternity. It was God Himself exacting this expiation by the abject taint each month." Her master assures her that going forward she need not fear anything of the sort. She would never again be considered guilty by nature. She will, of course, continue to be whipped, among other outrages and abuses, but only because she is so beautiful, desirable, blessedly arousing, out of love in some way, as a goddess who must be profaned to be honored. Vowed to the carnal pleasure of her owners, she has now become the object of their adoration.

167. The professor and his daughter, by mutual agreement, decide to inaugurate this transfiguration by some sort of pious image: Suzanne, kneeling indecently, naked, wearing her black blindfold, is going to stroke and fondle herself with both her delicate angel's hands, still bearing her slave cuffs, while another courtesan, the little Sexty, in the same get-up but without a blindfold, will whip her bottom until she begins howling under the successive strokes of the tapered leather against her tender flesh. Thus, the splendor of a martyred saint is brought to life before the bedazzled gaze of the

faithful, marvelously realized, thanks to the passion that the two actresses put into it. Gigi cannot help but fondle Suzanne's shivering breasts and her moaning lips. She interrupts her ordeal briefly to explore her sex as well: her clitoris and her vulva are soaking as a result of an intense orgasm. The cruel girl asks her, "Is it the whip that is making you so wet, you delectable little rag?" Without altogether emerging from the faint, trembling, she replies, "I don't know, Madam, if that is possible …" "Or is it shame perhaps?" "There's nothing shameful about being whipped by one's masters… I feel their pleasure flowing on my hands …" The punishment having resumed more intensely, as well as the plaintive cries of the victim who carries on masturbating, the father finally releases a flood of semen all over the face of the fallen goddess, which she is forbidden to wipe, not even her mouth.

168. To make sure she will not attempt to do so surreptitiously, Odile immobilizes her arms behind her back again, closely bound. And she performs the same operation on her eleven companions. They all still bear the three or four heavy chains that drag at their ankles. The time has come now, to drive the twelve young ladies, naked and chained, to their respective prison quarters. They all, without exception, have passed the entrance exam, but with a wide range of grades. Suzanne is among the ones who received the most compliments. Sexie, not in competition, remains free to move about, the clasp on her shackles undone, and has been dressed, summarily, in a very short shift of gold silk from Violetta's wardrobe (which doesn't even reach her pubis). The little girl is still holding her whip, swiftly driving any stray lambs back to the flock with a snap. Let us not forget that all the captives, except her, are blindfolded and cannot see where they are being led, to a well-deserved repose, or to new torments, for those who received the lowest grades: perhaps even to their imminent execution.

169. Drawing closer to the *fornax*, the temperature rises imperceptibly. On this count, at least, they will have no cause for com-

plaint. First there are the sultanes' chambers, Suzanne, Sissy, and Sexie, who are entitled to sumptuous and cozy rooms, of a kind that the latter two, certainly, have never known. The former, on the other hand, by her birth, is accustomed to luxury and to all desirable comforts. As for the chains hanging from the vaults, as well as from the numerous and various hooks and rings, there to allow her to be bound in bed in a variety of postures, or from the walls and columns, the young woman thinks them quite natural, given the particular uses to which her charms are to be put. She is no more surprised to find in the adjoining bathroom, vast and perfectly equipped as it is for bodily hygiene and aesthetic care, a torture trestle, winches for pulling limbs apart, a bronze stake in the shape of an erect phallus of worrisome dimensions, as well as assorted other cruel devices, whose penetrations and the subsequent injuries she will be forced to endure some day or another. But for the time being, it will do to leave her hands tied behind her back, and Odile, having odiously caressed her as she peed, chains her to the sumptuous bed by an ankle, so she can, if not wash her face or her sticky blond pussy, at least rest a little before the dinner, at which her master requires her presence without her having been allowed to tend to her hygiene in any way, entirely naked and chained.

170. Sexie is enchanted with her own beautiful room. She's dancing for joy. Having received sufficient encouragement to make her feel like some kind of favorite, she surveys the spectacular torture materials (that here too only complement the rich furnishings) with more curiosity than anxiety. Sissy, on the other hand, in the room next door, starts crying in apprehension as soon as Odile lifts her blindfold, all the more understandable as the trestle's razor-sharp blade is largely stained with blood, nicely imitated by a paint that appears quite fresh, as though a prisoner had just been tortured astride it. The ancient wall coverings are, moreover, eighteenth-century illustrations of very young women dying, executed by the

monstrous methods in use in the harems of the Ottoman Empire.

171. Odile, who is highly amused at seeing her so terrified, lets her know that such pretty tortures are quite common in this dwelling, where she will perhaps not live long... However, she should know that crying, other than on command, is forbidden, and that the mistress will therefore come shortly to punish her for this wrong. Sissy's tears redouble to the accompaniment of moving supplications. Odile, meanwhile, ties her to her bed, spread-eagled, her limbs akimbo, chained at the wrists and ankles for the merited punishment to come. And she fondles the inside of her delicious russet pussy as deeply as her intact virginity will allow, using, to make the membranes more amenable to extended contact, a rather dense salve, whose application on even the most reluctant subject promptly provokes prolonged localized pleasure, but that is vermilion with a strong scent of spilled blood, which she forces the prisoner to then lick off her sticky fingers. As a foretaste of what awaits her, and with the prior approval of her masters, Odile then lashes her young breasts three times with the whip left behind by Sexie. Three lovely red lines appear on the tender flesh, as the sultane howls in pain and desperate spasms shake her perfect body.

172. After admiring her a moment, stirred by lewd shudders and convulsions that gradually subside, Odile gives her an intramuscular shot in her pubic cushion, with a double dose of the "house" drug for molding perfect, permanently accommodating sex objects infused with a kind of servile, erotic happiness, which the professor and his pupil have decided to administer daily to the boarders at their prison, no matter how young. Gigi's loyal love doll must now conduct to their respective dormitories, first the six little girls, Crevette, Nuisette, and Lorette, who are seven, eight, and nine years old, to J1, then the three others, Rosine, Caline, and Sabine, to J2. These are classic boarding school dormitories,

bright and spacious with rows of iron beds with rounded black headboards decorated with gold flowers, wide enough to allow the girls to sleep comfortably on thick horsehair mattresses and metal slats. Each girl has her own night table with three drawers, one of which locks with a key that only the masters can unlock. On the walls, there are photographs of lithe little girls, generally naked, most often bound, being whipped by older girls, adult almost, and sometimes also naked, in various traditional or deliberately obscene postures. The bathrooms are communal, consisting of rows of sinks and showers, as well as Turkish-style toilet bowls without seats, with slightly raised steps, intended for the feet and further apart than usual, on which the little girls must squat, spreading their thighs far too wide.

173. These collective bedrooms, infinitely more comfortable and cheerful than the ones at the inquisitorial police complex where they were sold at auction, are also a great deal nicer than the huge dormitories at their disposal in the convent of sexual education, where they were also not spared the whip. Nonetheless, Sabine, the oldest of the arriving girls, whose twelve summers are accompanied by precocious signs of femininity (tiny pointed breasts and downy pubic fuzz) was no doubt hoping for an individual room, like those that had just been assigned to the courtesans, barely shapelier than her. Although she has never before enjoyed such a privilege elsewhere, the child displays her disappointment by an obviously sullen attitude. Odile reprimands her severely. "Your ill temper will surely merit punishment you poor, foolish girl!" In fact, the other five girls appear quite pleased, all the more so when the sub-mistress removes their heavy chains and slave irons so that they might gambol as they please and freely choose their beds, for they will be only three in a room intended for seven. So Sabine is the only one bound, waiting for who knows what. All of them, however, receive their dose of sensual enhancement, with which, from now on, they will be injected daily.

174. Rosine and Caline, the arrogant girl's two roommates in J2, point out to Odile the presence of four quite separate cells behind the water closets. Reserved unquestionably for girls being punished, these are isolation chambers whose structure consists entirely of vertical metal bars about ten centimeters apart. On the inside of these veritable exhibition cages, the bed is reduced to a single narrow plank on a hinge, clearly quite uncomfortable, one might even say impossible for use by a tall adolescent girl. The floor surface is barely two meters by two meters, of which the toilet bowl occupies a sizable portion. Identical to the others in its design, but differentiated by rings that serve to chain to footrests the ankles of a squatting, pissing girl, but above all by the short, oblique stake that will enter her anus, with some difficulty no doubt, given the dimensions of the brass knob in which it ends, like some monstrous testicle. This, moreover, is pierced by a large conduit at one extremity, leading one to suppose that it is used for the administration of revolting and cruel enemas under the beatific gaze of the other boarders.

175. Her two mischievous schoolmates find it very entertaining, at any rate, to assist the sub-mistress in placing their cranky co-captive onto this barbaric and indecent instrument. It takes all three of them and a good deal of patience and emollient ointment to succeed in inserting the ball of contention inside the hitherto inviolate sodomites' temple. Sabine fights while crying out in pain and indignation. When the girl child has finally been firmly impaled, and her feet restrained in a trying posture, Odile gives her a whopping slap in the face and orders her to shut up, now that she has obtained the private quarters she demanded on arrival and which her youthful beauty dictated. Next, she stuffs a huge plug in her mouth to muffle her shrill howling and reduce her entreaties to vague incomprehensible whimpers. Blood flows from her torn anal orifice, staining the stem of the stake, and the white enamel around it, red. Before abandoning her in this state,

as pleasing as it is shameful, for who knows how many hours, the blindfold is put back on her, which will blind her imploring eyes, where terror can now be plainly read beyond her tears.

176. Caline then tells Odile that she needs to pee. Her warden, amused, immediately understands the proposition and acquiesces: "Do it here then. That's what the Turkish-style toilets are for." The two little girls, chuffed, immediately stand right up against the prisoner: Rosine, from behind, lifts her face up and holds it firmly, while Caline, standing with her legs apart, positions herself in front of her in such a way as to direct the jet of urine toward her nose, the black band, her mouth, distended by the plug, so that the thick fabric is abundantly drenched with hot urine. It makes them both laugh, such a fun game. Wearing no panties herself, Odile would happily take part in this disgusting dousing, but deems it contrary to her dignity and her station. In her gold silk mini-dress, intentionally too short for decency, the improvised sub-mistress in whom Gigi has just spontaneously placed all her trust, having, herself, to supervise the brand new servants in the kitchen, avails herself marvelously well, all things considered, of her unexpected, utterly new duties, and takes a marked pleasure in them, concealing, as best she can, the sexual arousal it produces. She has yet to lead them to their dungeons—in this case individual ones— these four girls "sentenced to death," designated as such by the father at any rate, in truth, are not threatened by any such projected sacrifice, in the near or distant term.

177. The girls, as beautiful, innocent, and virgin as their nine cohorts purchased at the same time, accept the purely formal denomination without objection, all the more so since it is provisional, soon to be revised, they have been told, in particular in compensation of their merit. They are Christina (twelve), Pauline (thirteen), Octavia (fourteen) and Agatha (fourteen and a half). The aphrodisiac shot promoting erotic goodwill appears to have had an immediate effect on them, as the two oldest are kissing with a most

sensual ardor before parting, rubbing their naked bodies against one another, unable as they are to use their hands. Odile assures them that they will soon see each other again, their public frolics, along with other appropriate mistreatment, is liable only to please the masters. As a supplementary precaution, the sensible warden makes them visit dormitory J2, as an example, to observe the risks run by captives discontent with their assigned lodging. The notorious "dungeons" are, in actual fact, less frightening than decorative and, for the most part, symbolic, medieval-vaulted rooms with enormous hanging chains, heavy cast iron rings sealed in the rough-hewn rock at various heights, bedding of straw, massive stoneware jugs and matching troughs for grooming or meals, observation posts, and so forth. The whole lot is bathed in heat propitious to constant nudity, dim lighting (other than when the floodlights are on), and the oppressive scent of a love hole.

178. That evening, dinner would not be starting early so the participants might appear beautiful, rested, groomed, their hair arranged, wearing discreet makeup (on their lips, eyes, nipples, etc.) except, of course, the punished captives, Suzanne, Sissy, and Sabine, who would appear dirty, humiliated, weeping in shame, their hair disheveled, exhibiting their recent lash marks, or ignobly soiled, still bound by their leg irons, chains and shackles, an especially unjust fate in the case of Suzanne, now the master's favorite, who is guilty of no fault, not the least one, apart from being too beautiful in the eyes of everyone. This, she still is, moreover, in this new guise as the ill-treated slave girl, her face spattered with drying sperm, her fragile ass crisscrossed by sepia trickles of blood where Sexie's lash struck it too hard. Fresh blood is also flowing, though more abundantly, from Sabine's torn anus, the wound having reopened when she was unceremoniously yanked off the huge glans of the stake. The pretty vermilion lines on Sissy's very young breasts appear more clement in comparison. There are four gentlemen here to openly enjoy the vision of these girls (a bloody pussy with its sticky slit, the russet fur between a pair of thighs, onto which a

reddish juice is streaming, a sweet, quite sleek, apricot) in a row, kneeling and begging for mercy. The father, who had wanted them to appear in this state, is there, as are his three guests.

179. The prudent Gigi, to celebrate her pseudo-birthday, has actually invited Marco, the likeable policeman whose acquaintance she had just made at the special prison, to join them, as well as the Englishman, so competent in these matters, whose name is David Locke, along with his son Jonas, barely an adult, who has come with his fourteen-year-old fiancée, naïve and blond, familiarly called Babie, a bit stupid perhaps, but easy on the eyes, and no doubt more so to touch. Marco, for his part, has brought, by way of a gift, much as one might bring a bouquet of roses, a young virgin, thirteen and a half years old, pretty as a picture, who will be sacrificed for dessert. The female guests, other than Odile and Sexie, are the mistress's ancillaries, Agathe and Octavie, the two girls "sentenced to death" who love each other tenderly, as well as Suzanne and Sissy, the penitent sultanes, set free after being pardoned, so that they can go and clean up quickly, and return to the gala in their full splendor, completely naked and rid of their slaves' irons. Dinner is served by the five available little girls, also naked, whose chains at the wrists and ankles are replaced by much less heavy gold metal cuffs encrusted with semi-precious stones. They also wear dog collars with a pendant medallion specifying their age and first name. The blue color of its leather indicates their total virginity, back and front; Sabine, the sixth girl, too damaged by the stake, has to be sent to the doctor, who will give her soothing baths and a couple of stitches.

180. As was customary in her mother Violetta's days, Gigi wants to watch an edifying scene while the little girls serve apéritifs: the punishment of girls found doing something wrong: today, Sissy, the plaintive sultane, too lightly punished by Odile upon her arrival in a luxurious room, whom the injection has transformed into a sensual, consenting victim; almost unscathed, indeed al-

most blossomed by the lash marks on her delectable bosom, she has no trouble making herself look pretty and coming back promptly, unconcerned by what might be awaiting her. On the other hand, there's Octavie and Agathe, who responded in too lively a manner to being separated; it is sweet Octavie who will be punished, in both their stead, in front of her lover, whose own charms, sensitized by the shot and the drug, Gigi will be fondling to make her come while her beloved is being tortured. Finally Antoinette, Marco's slave, a professional of voluptuous cruelties, rounds out the trio of martyrs displayed. She can be tortured without restraint, as she must perish tonight anyhow. The mistress decides they shall all three be lashed viciously on their crotch and inner groin, hung upside down, their thighs spread wide, their hair flowing, their shoulders and neck only resting on the ground.

181. Swiftly, they are placed in position, an appetizing garland, each girl's foot almost touching her neighbor's, their hands bound behind their backs, showing off their love muffs of matching hues: a blond, plump where it counts, aged fourteen, a redhead who is six months younger and precociously pubescent, chestnut with shifting tints, whose promising delights (she's only thirteen and a half) consist of particularly ravishing little breasts and a still silky pubic fuzz. Antoinette, as well as Babie, who only speaks English, has been given double doses of the powerful aphrodisiac serum on arrival, subduing all attempts to resist, however understandable. Gigi suggests that prior to hanging them, as one might butcher's meat, for the undoubtedly undeserved punishment, the silent little lamb delivered by Marco to be sacrificed should be deflowered for practice by young Jonas (whose fiancée too, is a virgin). Four little girls promptly grab Antoinette, force her back against the edge of a couch, her legs parted, her knees raised to better offer her sex to immolation. Jonas barely caresses her, but Odile confirms her vulva is a little wet and holds a whip out to the boy who, mildly surprised, unstintingly applies himself to lashing the as yet unopened slit of the little girl, who soon is in tears. He

then impales her in a single move on his erect cock of, admittedly, rather modest dimensions. The little girl's first cry is followed by restrained moans of pain from the subsequently ample toing and froing of the blade of flesh. The spectators note that she's losing blood at each retreat, in laudable abundance. This further arouses her rapist who, feeling his discharge mount too rapidly, pulls out to stuff his blood-covered member in the mouth of this child, who is ordered to swallow it all. When, trembling in fear and half choked, she allows some sperm to drip out of her parted lips, he lashes her bloody vulva again, but with a heightened desire to inflict injury.

182. She howls in pain without daring to fight back. The little girls let go of her limbs to applaud. Antoinette, convulsed by sobs, returns to join the two victims waiting to complete the tableau. She is bleeding a great deal, though it is primarily due to her deflowering. The scarlet sauce is now flowing onto her belly, drowning her navel, all the way to the bottom of her still immaculate breasts. Her tears redouble when she understands her torture is to be resumed… And more cruelly, evidently. She hopes she will die of it quickly. Next to her, the blond Octavie also starts to weep softly, soundlessly. It's Odile who handles the whip, with her usual dexterity and clever variations in the placement of strokes, and also with varying intensity. She begins with Sissy who, for her part, wastes no time breaking into tears. Gigi feels the tableau has been very successful and compliments the actresses. Then, the attentive mistress herself gives her lieutenant directions as to who the next series of lashings will target, their number, their intensity, the precise point that the stiff crop must strike. The professor, meanwhile, is fondling Sexie, then Suzanne's pussy after she returns to sit to his left. Gigi is on his right, the child rescued from those who would flay her is still on her knees between her legs. When the director finally announces the end of the punishments, two of the flagellated girls are made to stand, they do so, just barely unsteady, go back to their place at the table, even though their arms

will remain chained behind their backs. One can see that Sissy has been relatively spared, only her inner groin is somewhat too bright a pink. Octavie is bleeding a bit, not excessively, at the top of her left thigh and in the dimple of her groin.

183. Antoinette alone remains on display, upside down, whimpering in a very touching manner. The lower part of her belly, her inner thighs up to the knees, and her entire pubic mound drip with fresh blood at her slightest feeble movement. Her moans redouble when Caline, the little ten-year-old whom Gigi has assigned to watch her, intermittently pours pure alcohol on her torn-up cunt, allegedly to disinfect it. Her moans then turn into cries of distress and wretched babbling, directed to her tormentors. The meal is very lively, due apparently, in equal parts, to the flavor of the dishes, the initial erotic episodes staged, and the alcoholic beverages that everyone is imbibing liberally: all one needs to do is signal one of the little serving girls to pour, they themselves have received orders not to drink too much surreptitiously, warned of disproportionate sanctions at the slightest sign of drunkenness. As for Sissy and Octavie, who must lean all the way forward to snatch a few morsels of food with their lips or teeth off the plate, it is a gallant, highly appreciated pleasure for those sitting next to them (Marco in the case of one, David Locke, the other) to bring a glass that is too full to their lips and tip it so they can aspirate what quantity of intoxicating drink suits them. After which (or at the same time), they fondle their breasts as compensation for their diligence in drinking without slurping.

184. David, having just finished a lengthy dousing of the desirable Octavie, whose fairness he is finding increasingly seductive, feigning a wish to wipe her luscious lips, kisses her on the mouth in a most convincing and quickly reciprocated manner. So, he slides a hand under the table to fondle her pussy as well. The girl immediately pulls back, though in a way that appears unrelated to modesty, given her apologetic smile. The man, however, feels his

fingers are entirely wet. Withdrawing his hand to look, his fingers are red with blood. He had forgotten this detail and regrets his move, having had no intention whatsoever of hurting her. Out loud, however, he remarks on the distinct discrepancy in the fate undergone by each of the accomplices, both guilty of the same crime: that of Gomorra. While Agathe was only artfully masturbated until she experienced a long series of orgasms, Octavie was savagely whipped on her delicate blond pussy, turned bloody. The plaintiff's demand meets with the audience's warm approbation, the lady presiding at this tribunal pronounces a verdict. After Gomorra, comes Sodom: hence, a well-equipped man shall demolish Agathe's pretty ass, inflicting as much pain as possible, while Odile whips her breasts, until she is bleeding satisfactorily.

185. The burly Marco will execute the sentence, he doesn't have to be asked twice. Agathe, whose wrists he begins by tying behind her back, is delivered to him. Then he kneels her on the edge of the divan, thighs quite wide apart; he leans her forward so she is presenting him with her ass and its spread sluice. His erect cock is huge, but with a bit of lubricant he buries it without any difficulty, with delectation, inside the anal orifice. The condemned girl emits a perfunctory cry, so feebly that the rapist is suddenly suspicious, "Has anyone fucked you in the ass before you little whore?" "No sir, I swear. A nun talked to us about this practice at the school for model wives, as it's something that gentlemen apparently often impose on their young spouses. We just tried it among ourselves at the dorm using raw carrots, and we talked about it to figure out if it could be something nice." "Well, it won't be today!" answers Marco, sodomizing her extremely violently. And to make sure she takes no pleasure, as a result of the libidinal pleasure injection, he lifts her upper body so Odile can promptly begin to whip her breasts with a thin cutting lash, handled with such vigor that the girl's delicate skin is torn by almost every stroke. The rending screams of the studious schoolgirl this time leave no room for doubt as to their nature.

186. When Marco abandons her, sobbing in her despair, her suffering, and her humiliation, one can see that not only is her splendid bosom bloodied, but that her exquisite rosebud too, is bleeding, ripped intentionally. Defeated and drained, she collapses to the floor. She begs to be given something to drink, and a little girl sets a bowl of water in front of her on the ground. The mistress says to her, "You were coming like a little bitch in heat a short while ago, now lap this up like a dog, go ahead, drink!" "Yes, Madam," the tortured girl manages to reply. "I'm sorry." As she has to pee, after the quantities of white wine drunk, while in Gigi's arms, in between her repeated orgasms, she is now made to piss while kneeling, her thighs spread over her water container, and to then lap up the mix of water and her own piss. It is decided she must be put on display in this state, cut up, front and back, bleeding and dying of shame, her wrists and ankles tied, mounted on a Saint-André cross, fitted at its center with a small oblique stake to be inserted inside her wounded anus in order to hold her body up in an X, preventing it from sagging.

187. Finding her so perfectly beautiful on her cross, where she stirs feebly, bound tightly by straps, Gigi immediately wants to try out the commercially banned ointment, brought by the invaluable Marco. Introduced inside the sex of any girl, even a very young virgin who has just been tortured, it immediately unleashes a torrent of such violent orgasms that she generally dies of them within an hour and a half, minimum. The police use it in their secret prisons as a means of execution that circumvents the laws forbidding capital punishment. This product is, moreover, harmless on all other mucous membranes, and therefore makes it possible to take, leisurely, one's time to fuck the supposed delinquent writhing in the throes of unbearable pleasure. Marco takes on the job of slathering it all over Agathe's vulva, her clitoris, and the entire area surrounding her intact virginity. A spectacular change comes over the girl being crucified within minutes. First, on her face, in the throes of a kind of dementia, her eyes widen, her mouth opening

in spasms. Then, her entire body is traversed by shudders, soon by convulsions. And very quickly there appear the signs of a sexual orgasm so intense, so acute, that it resembles torture. She must be given a shot in the throat to prevent her from crying out too loudly, which would disturb the dinner, once again resumed in a convivial, agreeable, though sexually charged, atmosphere.

188. The men all are busy with the girls next to them, or else having their cocks licked by a little girl kneeling under the tablecloth. Jonas would like his fiancée to strip, she is the only one of the girls not completely naked, with the exception, nonetheless, of the hostess and her faithful lieutenant. The boy complains to his father. David makes Babie come near to him so he can remove her panties. When she resists a little too vehemently, he slaps her and harshly orders her to take off her dress and everything else she is wearing, which, truth be told, is not much. The girl fears angering her future father-in-law: besides she doesn't mind showing off her brand new adolescent charms to the gathered company. She ends up complying with charming moves, of which her fiancé had not suspected her capable. Her very pale, blond hair matches the azure of her eyes; her modest pubic muff (which sees the light infrequently) is just barely more golden. But when she is altogether naked, hiding her eyes behind raised arms, in the falsely modest position of Phryne before the Areopagus, David demands she kneel, arch her back, and push her pubis forward between her very widespread thighs, to fondle her own sex using both hands. If she does not obey promptly, he will have her impaled by her cunt on a torture phallus, and whipped to death. The girl, panicked does as she's told, and one is inclined to believe the injection of the serum has had time to produce its usual effect, for Babie, who is only fourteen and still growing, begins to come in a way that surprises herself, even, more so her betrothed. But David demands she be punished for her hesitation before stripping, Sexie must whip her bottom while she continues masturbating, and the only moans allowed are those of pleasure.

189. Elected to execute this sentence, the little girl, in her enthusiasm to punish her elders, must have struck too hard, no doubt, because the English girl, unhappy and desperate, cannot hold back the tears of a lost child. Nonetheless, the tableau is judged so pretty that Gigi asks it be prolonged, ordering Sexie to apply the whip in a more clement fashion to the tender flesh, which according to David Locke, has never yet known the lash, a fact he finds deplorable. He is, therefore, delighted that she should be made to weep in this obscene posture, for it is the normal lot, to be anticipated by any young British bride from a decent family. The mistress, deciding to stage a less cloying episode at the same time, calls for the two "condemned" girls whose offerings the guests have not yet enjoyed, to be brought from their dungeon; Christina who is twelve, and Pauline, who is thirteen. Glad to be asked to join the festivities, the two little girls are frightened by what they encounter upon arriving: Antoinette, hanging by her feet, her sex in shreds, is covered in blood; Agathe, whose breasts have been lacerated by lashings, is writhing on her cross in an alarming manner; Babie is on her knees weeping while caressing her clitoris, while also being whipped on her ass from time to time. These new players, well rested, washed, carefully groomed, adorned to appeal, are entirely naked, wearing only the special prison irons on their wrists and ankles, their arms are chained together behind their backs. They turn gracefully so they might be appraised on all sides. At a signal from the father, Pauline, smiling, comes to kiss him on the lips. David caresses Christina's anus.

190. Disingenuous as ever, Gigi upbraids them for their late arrival. She orders, by way of punishment, that they should lick the blood off the two torture victims, to slightly clean them. Christina goes to cleanse Agathe's breasts with her tongue and Pauline, Antoinette's thighs and belly. "That'll be your dinner for the time being, and you won't be needing your hands." Babie, on the other hand, can return to her betrothed for dessert. But he asks that her hands be chained behind her back first, having found it very fetching on

the other girls. He will feed her by the spoonful himself, like the baby she has now become. The servile fiancée goes along. Under the double action of the serums and the lashing, she accepts, if not with pleasure, with perfect ease, her transformation into a compliant object of pleasure. Jonas takes advantage of this, as soon as she is seated beside him, to make her drink a full glass of syrupy wine, which she imbibes in its entirety. And finally, she recovers her smile, then an altogether childish laugh, delighted by her new status that is forcing the boy to constantly take care of her. Besides, having set the glass back down, he kisses her on her obliging lips while fondling her breasts, then masturbates their nipples, then soon her sex, which is abnormally wet. She is completely naked and defenseless, and this excites him. She spreads her sweet thighs further so he can furrow around more easily, since now she is his, whether or not her body wishes it. And the girl, barely surprised, feels rising, then invading her, her first ever orgasm.

191. Jonas, who is gazing at her, rapt, touches her ecstatic face with the tips of his fingers, then, abruptly, he gives her a slap, delivered precisely, but not too violently, only to better savor that this delectable thing that functions so well is fully his property. Besides, this is how Babie takes it, and she kisses him to apologize for coming in public with such a lack of modesty. Meanwhile, on stage, the two lickers have almost completed their task. Since they began, they could be seen from the back, one standing, the other kneeling, their legs slightly spread to maintain their balance. Their almost immaterially delicate hands, chained at the already bruised wrists just above their ravishing little bottoms, and Jonas, like the other spectators, wonders why no one is whipping them to heighten their zeal for the job at hand, it seems like the least of things. Gigi must have had the same thought, for now she wants Pauline to come and lay at the foot of her armchair to lick her vulva and, most of all, her clitoris, as Sexie, with adroit lashes, draws the same scarlet striations that adorn Antoinette's belly, now being washed by Pauline's saliva, on these adorable exposed

buttocks. The order is swiftly carried out. As for Christina, whose tongue has not licked Agathe's breasts with the same attention, she is placed in a squatting position over a hard, wooden horse, the sharpened ridge atop which will all the more easily enter her pubis as her feet are being pulled to the sides with short ropes, her arms remaining tied behind her back.

192. Gigi's piercing eyes dart exaltedly from one to the other: Agathe, her breasts branded in red, continues to come desperately on her cross, and will for another hour, should one wish to watch her die this way; Antoinette, hanging upside down, whose adolescent body, quite clean now, is embellished by bleeding gashes, artistically arranged by the adroit whipping from her knees to her navel, and who is to be executed this very night; Pauline, on the other hand, prone between the thighs of her seated mistress, diligently working, with her tongue and lips, on producing a progressive arousal in her parted quim. The good girl, sensually affected in turn, gives a slight start, contained as best she is able, each time the whip strikes, wounding her bottom with its leather swish, lightly slashing her skin. There is, finally, the young and sweet Christina, whose childish and sleek pussy is starting to suffer horribly, sliced in its median furrow by the sharp ridge of the rack. She shifts slightly when the pain becomes intolerable, but this, far from relieving her ills, only carves further into her mucous membranes, which are bleeding from the anus to the vulva. Her huge, abandoned eyes attempt, in vain, to mollify the no doubt sensitive, but capricious and cruel heart of this mistress who has all rights and appears to be savoring the tears clouding the eyes of this child, tortured without having ever committed a wrong, as she performs the expert nibbles on her clitoris.

193. Under the maddening influence of an imminent, portended orgasm, Gigi grabs the strawberry blond locks of the girl sucking her. Wishing to see Antoinette's blood spilled again immediately, she asks Jonas to leave his new toy for a minute, to rip the clitoris off

the young pretty girl he deflowered after first forcing her to submit to the lashing of her virgin jewel. The button of flesh, swollen with juice, delirious from the savagery of the multiple subsequent whippings, has acquired a purplish hue, easily discerned after the cleaning. When the thin pincers operated by her rapist proceed to the excision with all the recommended deliberateness, the victim emits hysterical howls as a fountain of vermilion sap gushes between her thighs. Jonas rams a rag tampon in her mouth, imbibed in her own blood, to somewhat muffle her insane cries. He then completes the sectioning of the love bud and, as the blood again inundates Antoinette, the gallant Englishman goes and presents his fiancée, as homage, with this blood-drenched trophy, which he places in her mouth so that she should swallow it, which action Babie does not dare refuse. "This is how," remarks the mistress, who has just been racked by a strange ecstasy as though thunder had transformed her body and her spirit enduringly, as though, inadvertently, she had penetrated another universe of delirium and hallucination… In a dreamy voice, she endorses Antoinette's mutilation, savored as dessert by Babie: "This is how a primitive young bride must act in the face of all her rivals, as would a ferociously jealous queen have done, in Pomerania, not so very long ago…"

194. It is then that she notices Sexie ramming white-hot needles in Christina's dainty feet, piercing them to the core with fiery bolts of lightening, making rivulets of blood stream down both sloping sides of the rack. Gigi thinks, fuzzily, that her father must have given this order, and the one to prop her mouth open with a gag drenched in her own blood. But here are two naked little girls coming toward the mistress to present, on bended knee, an immense silver tray on which sits the sumptuous birthday cake covered in pale pink frosting, its center adorned with redcurrant syrup, spilled in bloody licks every which way. On it, fourteen lit candles, and additionally, in the middle of the scarlet puddle, one half of a fifteenth, equally sized, candle, since the girl, that morn-

ing, had turned fourteen and a half. The electric light in the room has been dimmed progressively to accentuate the bright glow of the candles, which soon constitutes, since it is dark outside, the only light in the vast ceremonial dining room. Gigi, mesmerized, gazes speechlessly at the radiant faces of the two little girls shimmering in the flames, and she distinguishes all around, at a respectful distance, other young faces belonging to the many little girl servants whose numbers have grown, perhaps very rapidly…

195. Wishing to escape this terrifying invasion, Gigi, with a strong puff, blows out all fifteen candles. But as if she had, at the same time, turned on another lighting device, Antoinette's illuminated body is exposed on stage, ever more contorted, traversed by abrupt, searing convulsions. Someone (Marco?) has rammed a fireworks torch in her vagina, which is spitting sparkles onto her thighs and all around, as the flaming tar pitch flows down her thighs and belly. Quite quickly, the condemned girl is engulfed in flames. The company applauds in justified exultation, then, in a chorus, intones the *Ode to Joy*, whose celebrated notes conclude the Ninth Symphony, when abruptly, the sobriety of high-minded humanism is interrupted by a noisy ripple of happy giggles, a little inebriated perhaps, the laughter of little girls. Gigi, surprised, instantly identifies the source by the dazzle of a welcome projector light, the silver tray and its birthday cake have been set on the floor, around it six or seven kneeling captives, whose hands are bound behind their backs, are having the time of their lives, grazing on the enormous confection straight from its dish, smearing their faces with pink cream and thick redcurrant syrup… Very clearly, they are stuffing themselves more for the fun of it than out of hunger, making themselves as dirty as possible, going so far as to wipe their noses and chins on their neighbor's breasts. Gigi, for her part, does not find this at all amusing, she even feels nauseous in the face of this bestial and repugnant display, she wants to get up from her seat, but before succeeding, she collapses, depleted, utterly limp, having lost consciousness.

196. Shortly thereafter (how much later?), her father wakes her gently, and in his usual authoritative tone asks her to please follow him: there's something he must show her. Gigi has recovered a certain energy, as well as a tranquil sense of well-being. There is no one left in the great dining room, which is feebly lit, though in an altogether ordinary way. Antoinette's upside-down body has been charred to almost complete cinders, with the exception of her shoulders and face, which remain on the floor, inert, the flow of the tar-pitch flame having stopped at her breasts, which smoldered for a long while, though not as long as her lower body—positioned above them—that is, her belly, ass, pussy, and thighs. The professor points out the heady scent of incense wafting in spirals of bluish smoke, the very opposite of the repulsive aroma of burning flesh. The manufacturer of the ingenious product that charred the adolescent alive has taken care to spare the executioners' olfaction The cadaver will be disposed of in the police crematorium. He explains, moreover, that the apparently lifeless bodies of Agathe and Christina, fainted after excessive torture, but ultimately very lightly injured, have been taken, along with Sabine's, to the in-house infirmary. The general practitioner has confirmed that in less than a week no visible harm will persist apart from a few rare marks from the memorable feast, such as the burns made by the red-hot iron on the soles of Christina's feet. And it will be possible, again, to use the captives, all three as pretty as before.

197. Afterwards, holding each other's hands like lovers, they walk down to the ancient Roman cellars, restored in the Middles Ages, under the *fornax*, whose refurbishing Violetta had judiciously overseen. Gigi, lost in thought, had been unaware that there was a working infirmary here for the harem, and a doctor able to undertake minor surgeries. She dare not ask for how long. As soon as she reaches the place to which her father wishes to lead her, a room that is quite hot, almost excessively so, equipped with various complicated devices, intended for pretty girls sentenced to death, two of whom she sees mounted on instruments and await-

ing torture, completely naked, rigged in obscene or cruel positions, barely moving, and crying soundlessly. Given their youthful, perfectly developed charms, they must be fifteen or sixteen. Savagely, the professor reminds Gigi of her filial duty: she too, must immediately strip naked. What is she waiting for? Now that she is an accomplished and disabused sex object, he wants to submit her to a serious lashing before sleeping with her. "Forgive me, sire," she says humbly, "for not having thought of it myself, for forcing you to give me the order. But I do love obeying you."

198. Swiftly undressed, she kneels before him in the traditional pose: her hands behind her back, her gaze lowered, her thighs spread wide. He contemplates her with satisfaction, and she, in gratitude, receives the slap she has earned. He says: "Stand, I am going to tie you to the stake." "Yes sir." Gigi is very pleased. Her father has often whipped her, particularly in the course of their erotic reading sessions, but this is the first time that he ties her up. She deems she has become a more important, a more precious, a more desirable being. He shoves her toward a nearby pillar, her face is pressed against the hard and rough wood, which smells of old cedar, perspiration, raw cunt. In seconds, he has tightened a wide, supple leather belt around her waist, connected to the torture post at precisely the right height, narrowing her natural slenderness still further by an excessive tightening of the buckles, and he ties her arms together a little higher, each wrist held in place without any latitude against the crook of the opposite arm, barely higher than the elbow. Immediately afterwards, she hears the whip crack against the flesh of the other two girls. Gigi cannot see them, but she counts the number of lashes that fall on each victim, whose cries of pain or plaintive supplications she identifies without difficulty. She arches her back as far as she can, so as not to crush her delicate breasts against the dreadful pillar.

199. A few minutes later, her father comes back toward her and grabs her by the hips ... He then strokes his erect penis against

the soft crack of her ass as he tells her that soon it will be her turn, and that he will hurt her more than anything she has so far known. He will whip her until he draws blood. "You have every right to, Sir," she says tenderly, "I am your property." No doubt in order to place her in a position that suits his designs better, the professor moves a sort of very heavy, cubic footstool, made of cast iron perhaps, closer to her and forces her to set her right foot on it which is instantly trapped in a very tight sandal about thirty centimeters above the ground. She has, for this maneuver, to bend her right knee and push her other foot back to the left slightly, since her body remains tied closely to the column's axis at her waist. Her thighs have now been forced apart, very wide, asymmetrically. And she has to tender her hips toward the paternal hand that is fondling her anus, introducing into it a thick ointment, a lubricant no doubt, possibly aphrodisiac, very pleasant in any case, once he starts to masturbate her, with first one finger, then two. Next, he gives her a shot in the ass: "No reason why you too, should not benefit from the pleasure serum with which we have gratified all our schoolgirls." After which, he simultaneously masturbates her anal rosebud and her clitoris. Before long, the susceptible girl is ablaze, she is moving her ass in an as yet light swell, her vulva is soaked in juices, she begins to pant in a quite remarkable and progressively less controlled manner...

200. When her master deems her properly primed, he administers, without warning, four brisk strokes of the lash, so violently that she emits incredulous cries, identical to those of the adjacent girls, which is rather vexing. Barely seconds later, a smooth but very large object penetrates her welcoming, mistreated *menina*'s ass, which at present, is stigmatized from the searing slashes. The object penetrates with great ease, however, as it has been foreseen for this usage. It is, in fact, a Spanish *olisbos*, dating from the Renaissance, that her mother Violetta used to employ to demolish the nascent *eros* of virgin servant girls and to humiliate them publicly.

It resembles three large balls next to each other, separated by strangulations of ebony. The fourfold preceding treatment undergone by the adolescent girl, a submissive daughter to begin with—the excessive lubricant, the digital masturbations, the conditioning shot, the severe whipping—produce the anticipated felicitous outcome. The instrument's profound toing and froing, rapid or slow, with precise twists and a few shoves, to the accompaniment of classic obscenities murmured in her ear, quickly plunge the child into a purple paradise of uninterrupted orgasms, putting aside a few punctuating pauses.

201. She is on the point of exhaustion when the master releases her from the column and stool, still leaving her arms tied behind her back, however, with two of the dildo's balls retained inside her little deflowered ass. She is bleeding feebly out of three spots: her rosebud and two lash marks. He sits in his comfortable armchair and Gigi throws herself on her knees in between his legs, her avid mouth seeking his virile member through the gap in his black pajamas. He extracts the sacred engine himself, which, half-erect, to the adoring girl appears of monstrous proportions. After licking it from bottom to top three or four times, while lingering, with the tip of her tongue, on the brake to stiffen the stem, she takes the crimson glans in between her lips and pretends to want to swallow it. He advises her to perform her task as inexpert wife correctly, else he shall have one of the little girls brought to suck him to ejaculation while she herself will be whipped on her sex in front of them. The novice is clearly not ignorant of how to proceed: not only has she read numerous detailed accounts of various modes of operation in her schoolbooks and has had conversations on the subject with the professor, so as to acquire an understanding of his personal proclivities, but she has also often watched the thing performed by leased children, on guests or on her own father, in the course of festive dinners with friends held almost monthly. And to attempt it herself has been a recent temptation, but she had not

imagined that holding the sweet monster between her own cheeks would be so marvelous. Her professor, all paternal bias aside, is really rather pleased with such a perfect student.

202. From time to time, so as to interrupt the too-swift mounting of the final pleasure, he raises his daughter's torso to kiss her on the mouth, while pinching the buttons of her little breasts, or more often, and for no reason, to administer slaps after exploring her overflowing vulva. It would make him proud to share how well he has trained this child with a complicit witness. In the shadows of these diverse peripeteias, silent and watchful, is the young eighteen-year-old cook, Gilbert, Gil for short, a vigorous, handsome boy whom Gigi has noticed when giving her work orders. The father hired him recently on someone's recommendation, to serve as bodyguard, chief of staff, and harem guard, as well as executioner. At a signal, the young man approaches, surprised, but also charmed, to see our young, authoritarian mistress merely a step away in such an interesting position: entirely naked and prostrate, her hands chained behind her back, her mouth distended by her genitor's cock, her buttocks marked by a cruel lash, and a huge *olisbos* with balls stuffed deep inside her anus. So that she should understand quite clearly that this male who is lapping her up with his eyes, and whose deep and resonant voice she recognizes as, in effect, being the same as one with which, not long ago, she had engaged in an urbane flirtation, the professor gives him a few orders requiring answers. He thinks that this way he can make the girl feel she will no longer be anything but a vulgar sex toy, at the mercy of her father, whenever he wants her, an excellent way to cap her education.

203. This charmer, Gil, must therefore, starting now, proceed to perform the sacrifice, planned by the professor, of one of the exquisite victims who await, tortured this night to honor Gigi, an enticing embellishment to the instructive games she had played while a

studious little girl under the watchful eye of her sweet papa and tutor. Gil will himself choose which of the two condemned girls most appeals to him. With this particular aim in mind, he inspects them, first the one, then the other, on display atop the two torture machines conceived by Violetta for putting sultanes to death ten years earlier. She had drawn very precise plans for them, but her accidental death made their construction pointless, the atmosphere in the house having changed radically at the time, as had the rhythm of life. In the vast basement cherished by the deceased, barely accessible, the father had decided, nonetheless, some time later, to erect two projects based on her drawings as a monument to her memory. No one, until this night, has ever used them.

204. The first girl whom Gil examines is Maroussia: a fulsome blond of fifteen summers, sentenced to death by quartering in her native country, following repeated thefts of intimate jewelry bearing a luxury label, she is, as happens often to exceptionally pretty adolescents, sold for export as a virgin for torture, or as a plump chick delivered alive to gynebutchers. Here, she is exposed horizontally, about a meter below the floor, face up, her limbs akimbo, held aloft by a stake entering her foundation whose extremity, invisible inside her rectum, swells in a calculated response to animal heat, to the point where it can no longer be removed, nor penetrate any deeper. She is, moreover, suspended to the vaulted ceiling by a large belt of black leather tightened around her waist, identical to the one that held Gigi at her column. Her legs, spread apart, are being stretched divergently by two winches able to split them further yet, capable of dislodging the articulations, and of completely yanking them off even. Her arms too, are being pulled to the right and left, but bound more loosely. Her golden tresses fall to the floor around her tear-streaked face, which is half turned. On her inner thighs she bears the red marks, bleeding feebly in spots, of the whip the father used.

205. Gil delicately caresses her mouth, sensitive and carnal (she sweetly parts her lips), then her breasts, firm and full enough to remain erect in this position and not flatten, finally her blond pussy, whose moist slit is beckoning due to the splitting that has begun. She has, no doubt, been subjected to an injection of the serum too, because her clitoris reacts to the touch in a charming manner, her impaled condition notwithstanding. Introducing his fingers to her obliging vulva, the young man then assesses that she truly is altogether virgin, a detail that moves her sentimental punisher unexpectedly. He licks her clitoris at length and she begins to moan amorously. When the girl first saw this luminous young man appear above her, she thought he was an angel descended from heaven to deliver her. Gil, meanwhile, projects making the other perish so as to spend the night with this one until morning, to make her come as much as she would like, while whipping her from time to time and then, obviously, deflowering her. He kneels and kisses her on the mouth, lifting her head. Maroussia gives herself to him passionately. She barely knows thirty words of French but a few gestures suffice to make her understand that he will, this night, take her to his room. The face of the condemned girl lights up as if touched by a miracle.

206. The other girl, the one who now will be sacrificed, is called Nadia. Her limbs too, are spread in a Croix de Saint-André. But she is suspended vertically, her feet well apart, each set on a sort of narrow pedestal, very precariously balanced. In between her spread legs, a stake is erect, whose sharp point penetrates the sluice of her virgin cunt, without wounding it seriously. The palm of each hand, as well as the ankle of each foot (between the calcaneum bone and the Achilles tendon) are pierced by a steel rod whose ends are affixed to thin, very strong ropes that hold the body in a cross. But there is no question of the torture victim holding on to these in the event of a fall: she would only further injure her hands and feet. What presents the greatest danger for her is also the thing that is least visible: a flowing knot slipped around her neck, whose

still quite loose cord connects it to the vaulted ceiling, hardly discernible under her curly mane, which falls to her shoulders. If she moves a little too far and loses her balance, she will be hanged and, at the same time, impaled. The father has whipped her bloody ass, but he has been careful not to knock her from her perch prematurely.

207. This Nadia is a tall, slim girl with magnificent curves, and yet with the kind of svelte body without thickness or unsightly musculature. She's a creamy redhead, a virgin, she too, has been sentenced to death, but for less clear cause: disobeying paternal authority (in reality for having spurned the advances of her father, a clumsy, crude man). Gil is going to burn her tender delights with slight, then increasingly strong, applications, until he brings about her fall and its inevitable consequence. He will, to this end, employ a light lance whose end can be fitted with interchangeable iron tips reddened by the brazier's fire. After instructions from the father, who is containing his darling daughter's ardor to make him come as best as he can, Gil begins by inflicting multiple small burns on Nadia by grazing her breasts, her inner thigh, her armpits, her belly, her groins, the crook of her elbows, her thighs from the knee to her pinned sex, displaying a preference for those parts that appear most sensitive to him.

208. The lord and master of these premises (and of its entire female population) holds Gigi's head firmly and prudently in both hands, whether to distance her from the impetuous phallus as he directs the executioner's moves, or to again apply the voracious mouth, the fluttering lips and the little teeth that lack any aggression, to the end of the shaft or around the penis. But he can tell this perilous exercise can barely last more than a few minutes. On his orders, Gil therefore buries the red poker several centimeters deep inside one breast, then another. Nadia emits howls to which he puts an abrupt stop with a deep burn at the root of her neck and all the way to the larynx. Finally, he attacks the pubic mound,

beneath her sumptuous russet bush, and the faintly bleeding faultline whence peeps her clitoris. The victim can only emit a rattling sound, which only adds to her suffering ... Exhausted, vanquished, shaking, she allows one of the supports to topple, then instantly the second one, as the entire system is unleashed in the slow rhythms provisioned by Violetta. Her feet spread wider, the body descends progressively onto the stake, pulled down by its own weight, the cord tightens gradually around her neck. And then, everything stops, except for the flow of blood and the trembling of her flesh. Half-strangled only, not having ruptured any cervical vertebrae, her limbs stretched to ripping, the steel poker traversing her belly deep inside her womb, it will take her over an hour to die.

209. Facing away, Gigi has only been able to follow the sounds of this performance. The professor, however, having fully benefited from it, is stirred by the ingeniousness of his deceased child-wife. His long ejaculation begins right when a white-hot iron immolates the clitoris to the pubic bone, and once the entire system is set in motion. A large serving of spunk is then dispersed in spurts as far as the uvula of his daughter's little mouth, she religiously swallows everything in successive gulps. Half choked by the enormous paternal engine spitting its semen, the adolescent, breathing better as soon as this object is withdrawn, turns her gaze, while still on her knees, toward the fairy-like Nadia, who is in the act of dying for this, her happy birthday. The professor awash in extreme beatitude, and far from experiencing the bestial melancholy that purportedly follows every discharge, seems in fine fettle, smiling, relaxed, wanting to smoke one of his Havana cigars while contemplating the spectacle, so plastically beautiful, of Nadia expiring in this slow and cruel fashion.

210. He selects a supple golden *robusto* from the case given the previous evening and offers one to Gil, whose services have been

A Sentimental Novel

perfect. He furthermore invites him to follow suit when he humidifies the cigar, to enhance its aroma, in Gigi's soaking little cunny, which she presents without having to be ordered, raising one of her bent knees and opening her thighs as wide as she can. The precious tobacco cylinder penetrates, to effectuate a few turns in her vulva, laterally, so as not to take chances with her virginity, which the master is saving for other games, as he explains to the executioner. The latter, slightly stunned, having never seen such a thing, which he is told is quite common, as is the burning, though not too insistently, with the incandescent tip of a cigar, the areola of a child's nipping breasts, a child transformed into a pretty and properly docile whore, whose virgin jewel humidifier will remain available for the duration of the savoring of cigars, and who will, in due course, should her master wish it, offer her tits to be burned anew. She will wear the brilliant marks on her sensitive and grained, brown-pink areolas for several months, or longer even. They will be like diamonds encrusted in her breasts that will materialize the memory of an unforgettable feast, reminding Gigi that she did not dream all that happened on this night of delights.

211. The young man strives to respectfully replicate this customary, meticulous use of the living and delicate humidifier. For the entertaining torture to breasts, he must use Maroussia's tits, markedly larger but equally pleasing. Having divined the kitchen chef's scheme, the master informs him that he will make a gift to him of the delectable blond prisoner sentenced to death. She will be set up in one of the beautiful rooms for sultanes. Fed and lodged by the establishment, she will be his personal property and will, should he wish it, assist him with his chores. As for her erotic employment, he will have to settle for fellatios and sodomy. At least until her deflowering, to which pleasure, as with all sultanes, the father holds the exclusive right as well as, doubtless, to other precise, customary tortures that will in no way cause her permanent harm. Before, as after, she will be requisitioned, occasionally, to

serve naked at dinners for friends, where the only risk she runs is of being fondled, more or less obscenely, along with cigar burns or needles stuck in her breasts.

212. Gil hastens to deliver his providential prey, as he had promised he would. The generous benefactor explains the procedure he must follow in a few words: undo the buckles of the belt suspending the body from the Roman arch, as well as the cuffs at the hands and feet: then lift the prisoner in his vigorous arms while the simple click of a switch deflates the apple in which the stake terminates, inside her rectum. The young man then need only drop the beautiful slave thus acquired down in front of his own chair, on her knees, in the same posture as Gigi. She will thus remain between her proprietor's legs, who can conveniently caress her mouth or her buttocks, manipulate her awakened clitoris (she is already very wet), burn the areolas of her breasts, and humidify his cigar as often as he should like. The disciple imitating the master heretofore, the two men compare out loud, openly, the vastly dissimilar charms of their respective lovely females who naturally only have the right to remain silent, as well as the aromas secreted by their vulvas on the cigars, the professor insists on tasting Maroussia's as well, drawing thrice on Gil's *robusto* so as not to mix the subtle sexual aromas with those of his own. They would have liked to savor Nadia the redhead's cunt, too, while she was still alive, but the latter is quasi-pierced, and a Havana cigar, at this point, would only acquire the flavor of blood if introduced inside her.

213. The indecent conversation having been prolonged, it is now very late and Gigi is dropping from exhaustion. It is therefore she whom the handsome Gil must carry this time, languishing in his arms, all the way to the nuptial chamber where she sleeps every night with her father. He sets her in the middle of the immense bed known as the Sardanapalus bed, where she lies sprawled on her back, her limbs splayed, so the professor can rape her without

having to wait for her to wash, since this expert has just taught him to forbid the scent of soap on pussies, plainly contrary to the bestial instincts of desire, still more so where young girls are concerned. Next, he leaves to take Maroussia to her new prison, almost as luxurious, though much more modest in size, in the sultanes' section. Gil would like to be able to inflict on her the same exaction as those that master is presently indulging in with his daughter, but he is mistaken. Actually, the father has gone to pay a nocturnal visit to several other captives, while Gigi, without changing her position on the bed in any way, has sunk promptly into the soundest sleep, which, however, does not preclude the eruption, in dreams, of an immediate continuation of recent events.

214. She thinks she has just realized that she can no longer move: she is tied to the bed in a cross and leaning over her, her father, in black pajamas, is gazing at her with an expression that is preoccupied, severe, anxious even, or else reproving. He is holding, in his right hand, a large butcher's knife whose long triangular blade, shiny and stropped like a razor, ends in a finely honed point that is already bloodstained. He is preparing to introduce this weapon into her sex, which she can feel is entirely wet, no doubt with blood flowing from it. She wants to beg him, to apologize, but quickly realizes no sound at all comes from her mouth. And the father, the enforcer of laws, buries the knife several times, not exactly through the natural orifice, but across the entire pubic mound, under the nascent, chestnut fuzz. The sharp blade penetrates deeply each time, without encountering bone at all.

215. To the child's great surprise, these wounds showering down that make her bleed terribly, rather than producing the awful, feared pain, give rise in her to an orgasm, at first diffuse and light, then rapidly growing. She shuts her eyes, opens them again quickly, disappointed not to have yet reached ecstasy, only to find her father, who continues to hold the knife in his hand, is simply

cooking on a charcoal brazier very near the bed, although she had never noticed it before. Right next to him is Maroussia, in the same exact situation in which she found herself earlier, before Gil rescued her, that is to say impaled by her anus and suspended from the ceiling by a large belt constricting her waist like a pitiless black corset. Meanwhile, her hands are tied behind her back now, and this confers an even more remarkable shapeliness to her superb breasts: two faultless globes connected to her thorax by rather marked circular narrowing as impossible to deform as all the rest.

216. The girl's marvelous legs spread ever wider, split progressively by the rotation of the two winches, which although somewhat slow, is irresistibly powerful. The tortured girl twists right and left, as though in slow motion, and opens her mouth to howl in pain. But no sound at all emerges. The father takes this opportunity to carefully carve out her blond muff, thick and soft, leaving the raw flesh under it behind. He then sets down the knife calmly and presents the scalp to Gigi, holding it in both his hands: a long triangle of fur whose inferior tip splits in two so as to frame the pubic slit. He adjusts this bleeding trophy of Maroussia's into the same position on Gigi, who begins to laugh quietly at how well this loan appears to please her creator. But, presently, he can apparently no longer unfasten it, the two skins have been soldered as though by a successful graft.

217. With his efficient butcher's knife he now cuts off Maroussia's breasts, holding the spherical part in his large, slender, pianist's hand and delicately slicing the narrowing at its base with his other hand, the right one. But this is not in order to fit it on to his daughter's dainty tits, because he throws the slices onto the grill of his flaming brazier. He is preparing breakfast, as on any other morning, by cooking the still palpitating mammaries, instead of sausages. He turns them over with the tip of his knife and seasons

them with pepper and with salt. Gigi is very hungry and opens her mouth avidly to receive a large nicely roasted morsel...

218. This is when her father wakes her with a kiss on her slightly parted lips, between which he has slipped his tongue, which the waggish teen pretends to want to chew. This handsome black-clad man leaning over her clearly resembles the other, but this time, it is her actual father, agile, limber, and jocular, just as he was before she fell asleep a little while ago. "You've been sleeping like a log for the last three hours," he says, "you've not moved a hair!" He promptly proceeds to tell her what he has been up to while she slept. He first visited the older girls' dormitory, J2, to fondle Rosine and Caline, just under eleven years old, whom he finds pretty. They greeted him happily, thrilled by the unprecedented feast where they had both been such a hit, and he taught them with greater precision how to suck cock (his). As they were not willing to let him leave, he placed them in position for elementary Sapphic games that they had been too young to study in school. Next, a visit to the virgin sultanes, where he spent some time sodomizing Suzanne, who turns out to be quite responsive to anal pleasures.

219. Finally, he deflowered Maroussia, so she could, afterwards, be accessible to everyone. She was afraid and Gil had to hold her open like a rag doll, incapable of defending herself. He must remember to punish her tomorrow for her incongruous resistance, aside from which she did come very nicely, as a result of the afternoon's injections. Gil, on the other hand, promised her the lash for her shameful displays of a bitch in heat. "You probably like her big breasts?" Gigi says, looking sulky. He confesses, with a smile, his preference for tinier pigeons, still in their nest. The adolescent turns her back but not so as to avoid contact, since, moving her back against him, she gently moves her bottom over the black pajama on exactly the right spot. "Touch me, please," she murmurs

tenderly. Sensing the open road, he simultaneously masturbates her clitoris and her anus inside which he again stuffs the precious love ointment. Her rose seems to him somewhat enlarged, actually, since he has no trouble burying his member in it in place of fingers, penetrating it all the way.

220. When Gigi wakes up completely, quite late that morning, she realizes her father has already left the master bedroom. She feels calm, rested, barely a hint of lassitude, happy with others, as with herself. Remembering the philosophical meditation where Descartes signals the sleeper's difficulty, after a long sleep, to clearly distinguish between dream and reality, she gets up and goes, altogether naked, to look at herself in the dark mahogany Empire cheval glass on swivels, bought by Violetta. She is quick to admire her own seductiveness from head to toe. What's more, no one has scalped her pubis, nor cut off her breasts, which appear to have grown, even. Instead, on their brown-pink areolas she can clearly discern five brand new burns caused by the paternal cigar. These bright red candies are very sensitive to touch. Their presence is indisputable, the same goes for the lash marks on her bottom. She puts a hand between her thighs to reach her rose of Sodom, at the base of the median. It is humid and viscous even. She looks at her fingers, there is ointment but also sperm, along with trails of blood. From all this, the burns, the lash marks, the bloody jizz, she extracts a legitimate pride.

221. On a folding table, her father has left the breakfast he has prepared for her: a Thermos of hot coffee and slices of quite rare roast beef that seem sliced by a razor. There is also a jewelry box containing a sapphire mounted on an engagement ring of white gold, and most importantly a short love letter with just the right dose of tender and lewd references. She decides then that she will no longer be called Gigi, which is far too childish, but Gynée, a word by which the Greeks designated young women of the age

to be devoured. And now she must go on her rounds to inspect the servants, as well as the various captives in her harem. Walking across the formal dining room, she notes that the great room has been cleaned and put back in order. The only remnant of the nocturnal feast is the heavy ebony trestle on which Christina was tortured. It will require at least two strong men to put it back in its place. The two upper sides of the trihedron still exhibit reddish drips that are in all evidence half-dried blood, not red paint, apocryphal or decorative.

222. In the main kitchen, the handsome Gil is busy with a great big butcher's knife, cutting thick slices off a heavy, bloody, block of meat. Seeing the young mistress, now in an elegant black dress, long and austere, he does not quite know how he should look at her after their night's adventures. Gynée asks where the chunk of meat comes from, which on one side has the whiteness of a girl's skin. "It's Nadia's buttocks and upper thighs, that splendid redhead tortured yesterday, that the professor told me to make a roast with it." Gil regrets that he cannot serve the breasts and the vulva, considered choice morsels at the special brigades cafeteria where he began his career at fourteen, as a kitchen boy. Had he known they'd be eating the girl, he would not have made her delectable charms irrecoverable by burning them as profoundly with the red hot poker, "right when your father made you swallow..." He brusquely stops in the middle of this ill-advised sentence, suddenly utterly absorbed by his work. "Made me swallow what?" Gynée asks glacially. "A liqueur, it seems to me, that he had produced himself." The young cook finishes his sentence, understanding that here reigns total oblivion of certain matters. Gigi-Gynée relaxes abruptly. She appreciates the fact that the pretty boy is not only a good cook and an adroit executioner, but also that he is capable of intelligent pirouettes, in order to extricate himself *in extremis* from a misstep. Again in a friendly voice, she asks if he is happy with Maroussia. "Simply put, I am hopelessly in love."

223. After her visit to the kitchens and outbuildings where she takes care of various household issues regarding the staff, Gigi-Gynée, or more simply Gyn (pronounced the American way: Djinn) goes first to Maroussia's room, the girl who under other skies had been condemned to die, provisionally on reprieve in the harem of little girl prisoners, and deflowered last night by the master. She is waiting, naked, in her pretty room, as is customary, washed, groomed, perfumed. She is flipping through a picture book for teaching basic French to young foreign whores, which consists of a great number of licentious terms, alongside matching drawings. She stands politely at Gyn's arrival. Like the rest of the girls, she know this pretty adolescent, barely a woman, is the all-powerful mistress, notwithstanding her state of sexual servitude vis-à-vis her own father. Djinn submits the new recruit to an attentive inspection, ordering with the use of gestures when her words are not understood. Maroussia turns again and again gracefully, spreads, bends, surrenders, etc. As anticipated, she has been whipped on her pussy by her owner, Gil, to punish her for coming so intensely in the professor's arms. Her russet mound is very arousing and she truly does have breasts that are as exceptional as in the mistress's dream.

224. She handles them at length with real pleasure, perhaps a bit of jealousy too, in any case intending to cruelly debase their splendor, without damaging them, however. The sultane having herself knelt, she receives the lash on her tits and their areolas, this on the pretext of making her expiate for her, needless to say, useless attempts at escaping the first rape. She tolerates the lashing without losing her pliant slave's smile, keeping her hands in the air and her thighs spread wide. She opens her mouth only slightly wider at the most burning strokes of the whip, which to a sweet object of carnal love are not unbearable in the least, but simply provoke a pleasant shuddering that traverses the body. Djinn asks: "Are you happy here, you little whore?" Her prey answers in a low and rather lovely Slavic accent deforming certain syllables, making

them almost incomprehensible: "Yes Madam, thank you for having kept me." And immediately, a radiant flush of affecting sincerity illuminates her young face. Very pleased with the interview, the inspector thinks that Maroussia will attain the highest rank at the intimate dinners, as well as during the sumptuous illicit feasts.

225. Next she goes to the infirmary where two slightly injured girls are receiving follow-up care, Sabine and Christina, each twelve, the former barbarically punished, the second, tortured for pleasure. The German surgeon is a handsome man of about thirty, named Morgann, kind and brisk, whom the young ladies find very attractive. So, he is treating Christina's split groin and Sabine's torn anus. He is treating them, moreover, to actively develop their erotic maturity. Both girls appear happy to be spoiled (and fondled) in the large, sunny room where their beds are. Agathe, for her part, who seemed dead when she was brought in here, hardly damaged, was, in fact, in a very superficial coma and has already returned to her dungeon. She has been given permission to see Octavie because they love each other ardently. Only, their hands are tied behind their backs so they don't do anything stupid, and one foot is very loosely chained to the great iron ring at the floor. Djinn comes across them kissing, rubbing just the buds of their young breasts against each other (on Agathe's there are fine cuts that have already closed up). They are on their knees facing each other on the golden, soft straw of the dungeon, an adorable pair of lesbians awaiting torture. They raise themselves nimbly at the arrival of their jailor in chief and assure her that they have never been happier.

226. The same is true of the little English fiancée who is also discovering love. Djinn talks to her in David Locke (her future father-in-law)'s room, where they slept together and are, at present, having a hard time parting. Upon the express request of his son Jonas, David sodomized the innocent virgin, taking a thousand precautions, several times, in various positions, and succeeded in

convincing her of the advantages of the practice, on the one hand for orgasms, but also to guarantee perfect virginity. He must now return to his properties, but he is leaving his daughter-in-law, delighted to have her perfect her education and serve as an actress at enchanting feasts such as the one held the previous evening. Jonas, her future husband, slept in eleven-year-old Sexie's bed, in her exclusive sultane's quarters. He respected her virginities, but they had great fun together, the way curious and sensual children do. Marco slept with Odile and they made love conscientiously, in a number of ways, very happy with each other. Gil, having punished Maroussia, whom he left in tears in her pretty room, spent two hours with Pauline, before going back to his prisoner to console her, utter a thousand gallantries, and make her come as sweetly as if they were ordinary newly-weds.

227. Gil and Pauline, in another world, are of an age to embark on their engagement, then head to church, as photographers bedazzled by their magnificent youth click away taking their picture. Decidedly, they noticed each other during the feast and several times exchanged enticing glances. Pauline is only thirteen and a half, but can boast a precocious sensuality, blossoming since the previous day and receiving the harem's psycho-chemical treatments. Among the adolescents with the most promising figures, she has, until now, been relatively spared. The scarlet striations decorating her pretty ass have not necessitated a doctor's intervention. In addition to loving glances, she gives the boy the number on the door of her dungeon.

228. So there he finds her, quite late that night, lying naked on her bed of golden straw, which pleases Gil and puts him in mind of inflicting on this conquest an entertainment that used to be in vogue at the Ethics Brigade: hanging a girl by her widespread legs from chains intended for this sort of thing, her shoulders and head alone resting on the ground, and forcing her to pee on herself in the pose. But first he lies on top her, kisses her and fondles

A Sentimental Novel

her clitoris and her anus so well that, ever more disarmed, she ends up complying with her lover's wish (who does not have the right to penetrate her) all the more easily, as there was no shortage of drinks imbibed with the meal, the elimination of which is not yet complete. Gil, therefore, chains her to the vaulted ceiling by her ankles and raises her upside-down body with the winch, hands tied behind her back; and he then obtains, while caressing her in this unusual pose, the best orgasms she has known. Immediately, with a fine needle chosen among the instruments of torture at his disposal, he pricks her pubis with its fuzz of brown silk, and her vulva that is streaming with cum, twenty-odd times. The charming pee soon splishes and spreads all over Pauline's body, who abandons herself, unrestrained, to pleasure, all the more so since her admirer, here, puts a stop to his reminiscences: at the Brigade, they would have proceeded to cut off the victim's clitoris, then naked with blood streaming between her thighs she would serve cocktails in the mess where, if the vermillion spring threatened to dry up, other fragments of her pussy would be ripped off with cutting pincers: the little lips, the tips of the larger ones, the muff and all its skin, as well as the tips of her breasts.

229. As for the three youngest little girls, Crevette, Nuisette, and Lorette, seven, eight, and nine years old, they really had fun serving. Brought to their dormitory, J1, they talk about it, dazzled. They were allowed to taste liqueurs that they served on their knees. They sucked off vigorous gentlemen and nice-smelling young ladies. They were caressed, kissed, licked. Arousing creams were stuffed inside their childish little orifices prior to masturbating them very gently. They admired an adolescent girl ablaze like a torch. They saw sperm and blood flowing, but also the tears of tortured girls. Towards the end of the night, they went downstairs to the caves to watch the torture of a thirteen-year-old servant girl (sold by her family) who had drunk too much. After raping her in every way, the gentlemen proceeded to quarter her on a special device, while sticking needles all over her body, whose four limbs were gradu-

ally torn apart. Finally, one of her thighs was yanked off altogether and she was left to die writhing in a torrent of blood, just like that. Oh yes, it was truly marvelous.

230. Lingering before going to bed, for they are not sleepy, they notice the door to their dormitory is not locked. They conclude after some discussion that, in this house where everything is regular as clockwork this is a sign that they have the right, tonight, to walk about freely. The premises appear deserted to them. They climb a staircase of stone inside a tower, all the way to an attic under the roof. There was no risk of any adults turning up here, as the roof, for the most part, is less than a meter from the floor. The little girls themselves, in spite of their diminutive size can only move about on their hands and knees. It's merely a place to pile away old books of no interest and mediocre carpets, threadbare in parts, and split and torn. No nocturnal lighting has been foreseen. Through a skylight that would allow a workman access to the tin roofing, a crescent moon can be observed whose pallor casts a vague, bluish light here, just sufficient to distinguish a book from a carpet. The three children decide this shall be their reading room, as the heat produced under the tin in the summer would forestall physical activity. Fortunately they are entirely naked. They lie on the ground on their backs after rolling bits of carpet out on the uneven wood slats. Lorette declares that she will read first. It is so dark that no one can tell whether or not she is holding a book in her hands. And she makes up a cock-and-bull story, which is just fine, given the kind of night it's been.

231. Trawling fishermen in Newfoundland often catch little girls in their nets. They are the same size as seven- to eight-year-old human children, but can only survive in salt water where they swim and jump like fish, which they are not either: their bodies have no scales and are warm, a little warmer than ours even, in spite of these very cold seas where they are commonly fished. As soon as they are captured, incapable of using their legs, which are remark-

ably agile in a liquid medium, they remain still on the bridges of ships in the bright sun of arctic summer, their backs to the ground, their pretty white and pink bodies shivering hopelessly under the delighted eyes of sailors, as they emit long, desolate plaintive cries that resemble our crying. To keep them nice and fresh until disembarkation they must be thrown into onboard fish tanks along with the rest of the sea creatures that are best sold to customers while alive.

232. Zoologists have studied their customs. They live in happy groups and feed on little fish that they catch by hand with surprising dexterity. They don't speak any articulated tongue, communicating among themselves in a kind of very musical song, enchanting but without any detectable words. This has led to the conclusion that they are a kind of small mermaid, even though the presence of four limbs clearly differentiates them from the Danish variety, much more current where we are from. They never grow into adults and their reproduction has remained a mystery. The most widely held opinion in this regard, is that they multiply by a sort of parthenogenesis, laying eggs like fish, but not fertilized, without there being true coupling nor a simulacrum thereof. As if, in spite of their graceful, attractive appearance, they cannot be young human females, they are sold at very high prices to Japanese consumers who appear to be very keen on them.

233. As they are nothing but heavy trawlers, although limited in capacity, the boats carrying this special cargo cannot attempt such a long crossing. The little girls must therefore be flash-frozen where they are fished, or in the immediate proximity. Their first stop is the Baffin territories, where enormous modern factories have been set up. They are, in effect, frozen at the very low temperatures used for conserving embryos. And it is important to avoid deteriorating their delectable flesh by progressive cooling; within seconds one hundred and thirty degrees below zero must be attained, and this without removing the subjects from their particular medium,

the perfectly limpid sea waters. The precious girls are transported in individual, cubic blocks of ice, around fifty centimeters on each side, so transparent that they can be very clearly seen inside in various poses, more or less curled up, in order to take up the least amount of space in the frigorific cargo. They have however, retained, following the abrupt petrification, their lively and amused gaze, an alert look, their lips slightly parted in a sweet smile.

234. They actually remain absolutely alive. And were one to thaw them according to the rules upon their arrival in Japan, they would once more begin to swim, laugh, and sing, promptly upon being immersed in the framing basins where they are placed, waiting, at the disposal of buyers who come to select them. The wholesale fish merchant then delivers them to rich gourmets, who all have their own fish tanks, in a fishbowl-van equipped to sustain their survival systems. Prior to a festive dinner, guests come to watch them play in the basin adjacent to the kitchens. To prevent them from devouring the smaller fish stored there, their hands are tied behind their backs, which does not appear to bother them as they swim around kicking just as naturally, lithely, and quickly. When they are hungry or simply playful, they move to the edges were visitors hold out sardines and anchovies, which they grab as they swim by and swallow without chewing.

235. Inevitably, the prettiest, who are being prepared to be plunged alive in boiling water, or held over a grill until they no longer move, first serve pleasures other than those of the table. As these nymphets offer three orifices for pleasure, deemed very exciting due to their narrowness and virginity, similar in every way to those of young Japanese girls who have been profaned for centuries, with or without their consent, everyone may rape them according to their proclivities, always provoking the same harmonious weeping, punctuated by cries of suffering, to be savored with delectation. It is even a fashionable indulgence to offer them as apéritifs to the debauchery of gentlemen who have come here to eat them.

But it is not possible, before cooking them, to leave them outside of the water too long as their marvelously soft skin dries, ruining both their sexual appeal and their gastronomic value.

236. This story over, Crevette, the youngest, declares that she would like to taste some wild little girls, but wonders if, in our country, any live ones are to be found for sale. The storyteller replies that here, in principle, their sale is forbidden for any use whatsoever, despite the fact that they use a type of language that has nothing at all in common with ours. Of course, there are clandestine clubs with Japanese restaurants, separated by a glass wall from a vast aquarium. Customers at the tables can, beforehand, enjoy twirling feats performed by the adorable little sirens that are going to be sacrificed for them. A collaboration with the police is naturally indispensable. The third child, Nuisette, declares, in conclusion, that in the so-called "normal" universe where they used to live, before being sold as objects of pleasure, everything that is fun is banned.

237. "Consuming wild little girls, in this or some other way, killing baby seals to steal their fur, eating foie gras, getting off before the bus or train has come to a complete stop, making love before the legal age, exciting one's papa by rubbing oneself up against him naked, playing with locks, making your pee splish-splash in an assigned urinal, raising Andalusian dogs, hunting this or that variety of deer, having dirty dreams, lending out your intimate assets in exchange for money, whipping servants or burning the tips of their breasts, using a girl's cunt as a humidifier for cigars, describing one's libido with great attentiveness, etcetera, etcetera..."

238. When Djinn arrives in dormitory J1, she finds her father there giving three little girls a good hiding for their escapade. They are naked, obviously, kneeling at the foot of the three adjacent beds, their hands raised against the Spanish ironwork to which their wrists are tied. They are, in this manner, exposing their delicate

little already rounded cheeks to the professor's whip, which strikes them one by one, multiple times, lightly to be honest, but making his supple leather lash snap against itself to produce the impression of severe punishment. The little girls emit feigned cries of pain, intercut with laughter that they do not even attempt to hide. When he unties them, laughing himself, the mistress asks what they could have been doing in this attic without electricity. Nuisette, the youngest, is the one who answers with her comically serious air: "We ate Japanese schoolgirls covered in burning caramel in which they had been dunked alive before our very eyes. It was very good. But they were dying far too quickly, we ought to have watched them wriggling for much longer."

239. Giving up on making any sense of this, the father and his cherished daughter, his pupil, his creature, kiss amorously. The girl, in a tender murmur, asks: "Did we, this time, commit incest and sodomy last night? What do you think?" "This," he answers, "appears to me divinely incontestable... Is there anything more that you would like at present?" "I don't know, Sir..." she says, hiding her face against the chest of his black pajamas. The three little girls, whose bottoms do, all the same, bear visible red marks, holding hands in a ring around them, begin a slow circle dance, almost immaterial, pensively dreamy.

Thus shall we forever live in celestial fortresses.